Demon Thingy

Book 1 – A Couple o' Conjurings

Jonathan Butcher & Matthew Cash

A BUTCHERED FOR CASH PRODUCTION

2017

DEMON THINGY

Copyright Matthew Cash/ Jonathan Butcher 2017

Edited by Jonathan Butcher

All rights reserved. No part of this book may be reproduced in any form or by any means, except by inclusion of brief quotations in a review, without permission in writing from the publisher. Each author retains copyright of their own individual story.

This book is a work of fiction. The characters and situations in this book are imaginary. No resemblance is intended between these characters and any persons, living, dead, or undead.

This book is sold subject to the condition that it shall not, by way of trade or otherwise, be lent, resold, hired out or otherwise circulated without the publisher's prior consent in any form or binding or cover other than that in which it is published and without similar condition including this condition being imposed on the subsequent purchaser

Published in Great Britain in 2017 by Butchered For Cash Productions, Walsall, UK

DEMON THINGY

What they're saying about Demon Thingy:

'An exciting fantasy novel penned by perverted morons who have somehow managed to be entertaining... for once' – Keith K. Keithly, author of 'Being Keith.'

'Like a crossover of early Pratchett, a bawdy 70's Carry On film and the court proceedings of a sex pest'. – Dan Billing, author of 'How Many Cats Fit in an Oven.'

'A highly entertaining fantasy novella with a twist; that twist being it's ridiculous, greasy and perverted.' – O.P. Yewtree, author of 'The Man with the Child in His Eyes.'

If Butcher and Cash were asked to write a satanic horror that's a cross between 'The Exorcist' and 'Bottom', then Demon Thingy would be it.

I laughed so hard reading it, that I spurted beer through my nose whilst making a mess in my trousers! - Paul B Morris, author of Within Darkness And Light, and founder of Nothing Books

1

Mrs Delia Roberts sat in the flower-printed armchair and watched as something shadowy unfurled in the corner of the lounge.

Drumming her knobbly fingers on the armrest, she heard her husband moan peacefully in his sleep upstairs: "That's right, Clive ... mmrrzzbb ... spread 'em wide ..."

Mrs Roberts' blasted arthritis was jipping her hands and spine something rotten, but the jipping underneath her bloomers was of far greater concern. It had been *far* too long since that particular itch had been scratched, nibbled, and gently strummed.

She had the lights low and the TV switched off, despite ITV currently screening the second of a three-part drama she'd been watching about transgender asylum seekers. Moths, butterflies and ladybirds danced in her tummy. She hadn't

DEMON THINGY

even bothered to dust around the back of the brass clock or hoover the place this time – she was feeling rather too impatient and more than a little miffed.

She had, however, still dressed her thin, ageing frame in a slinky nightdress, rouged her cheeks and waxed her legs, pubes, and upper lip.

The thing in the corner unfolded further, darkening until it was a silhouette that almost reached the ceiling.

It had been months since Mrs Roberts' last visit from the Great Old Horny Bastard. Normally she'd feign ecstatic wonder at the strange unfolding of an infernal embodiment of pure evil, but she wanted to make a point.

No one, not even the Archduke of Hades, had the right to keep Mrs Roberts' libido waiting.

"I CAME FOR YOU," something growled, as muscle-strewn legs appeared from the void and an exquisitely chiselled abdomen knitted itself from the fabric of reality.

DEMON THINGY

"Already?" Mrs Roberts muttered, her fingers fussing in her lap. "Well, you aren't going to be much use to me if you popped your load before you got here."

Arms sprouted from the black ether, the left one nudging a bookcase and unsettling one of Mrs Roberts' Faberge eggs which was balanced on the shelf. In symmetry, the bearded black head of the Dark One grew from the nothingness and a snakelike tallywacker unrolled between its legs.

"What time do you call *this*?" Mrs Roberts demanded.

"DELIA," the beast grizzled, the word penetrating the room like a curse. "I AM HERE TO TAKE YOU TO WHERE YOU BELONG. TO TAKE YOU ... DOWN."

Mrs Roberts sat up. Her back gave a twinge. "Now?"

The beast – 7 feet tall and built like the proverbial – stepped forwards. Its musk was like a dog being barbecued in a barn. "SOON. BUT FIRST, YOU MUST COMPLETE ONE FINAL TASK."

DEMON THINGY

Mrs Roberts sagged back into her chair.

"YOU MUST CLAIM OWNERSHIP OF THE COVEN. SHOW THEM THE TRUE PATH."

Now *that* was quite unexpected. Mrs Roberts considered her fellow demon worshippers, and wondered how challenging it might be to take control. It might not be too tough, what with that incompetent twit Lady Saffron stumbling through the occult rites at every meeting. That woman barely knew the difference between Beelzebub and a bumblebee.

"And if I do this, I can live in hell?" Mrs Roberts asked, trying to keep the glee from her tone.

"YES." The beast stepped closer.

"At your side?"

"YES." It was only feet away now, and its coal-dark flesh glistened.

"As your one and only bride?"

A pause.

DEMON THINGY

"CLAIM THE COVEN IN MY NAME."

"I will."

The beast reached down, pulled her close to the runnels of its stomach, and wrapped her in its arms.

When it began to push the top of her head down, Mrs Roberts said, "Oh alright then but let me take my teeth out first."

DEMON THINGY

2

On the morning that Seamus found the book – which led to events that would plunge the world into the gravest apocalyptic danger since Kim Jong Un spilled donut jam onto one of his reddest buttons – Seamus was disappointed at the lack of drama. There was no creepy Asian shopkeeper at hand, offering him a veiled warning against the horrors to come. There was no dramatic flash of lightning, or ominous music, or a set of obscure rules he was advised to live by regarding his purchase. There was only a slightly cross-eyed, acne-coated teenager slumped behind the shop counter, staring at the screen of his mobile phone while rubbing his genitals through his trouser pocket.

"Young man," Seamus called. "Young man, how much are you selling this for?"

DEMON THINGY

The pizza-faced penis-pumper looked up at the book Seamus held. He offered a slothful shrug.

Must be new. Seamus was used to a more respectful style of response. Most occultists and sellers of mysticism recognised that Seamus's pointed grey beard, battered fedora and long, shabby robes reflected the fact that he was, as they say, "The Real Deal".

Seamus had been happy that this little shop had recently opened, because there weren't many purveyors of occult mysticism in Walsall. The room was fittingly cryptic, with its animal skulls, body parts in jars and atmospheric candle lighting. The books were typically dusty and sacrilegiously titled, the blades and wands all either elaborate and deadly or menacingly minimalist, and eerie trinkets were piled in random-looking arrangements, giving prospective customers the sense that they might stumble upon quite literally anything while perusing the room's oddities.

DEMON THINGY

So why was that dopey-looking public masturbator who was slouched behind the till lowering the tone?

Seamus grumbled and lowered the sleek witch's blade he'd momentarily been interested in. He stroked his beard, from chin to pointed grey tip. If this blotchy twerp had no interest in providing the right service to an esteemed member of the occult community, well then, Seamus would take his business elsewhere. He turned, preparing to huff and stomp an unimpressed exit, when a red book halfway down one stack caught his eye.

Under Seamus's trousers, a chill that he had only experienced once or twice in his long life scampered over his skin. He assumed that, had he been a "complete man", he would have achieved a rather impressive erection, but those days were banished to history. Seamus reached into his pocket, retrieved a cashew nut from a half-eaten packet, lifted his robes and popped a nut into his anus to calm his nerves.

Delicious.

DEMON THINGY

Then he extended an arm and listened for the telling crack of thunder that would signify an unearthly discovery.

Outside the glazed glass of the shop door, someone yelled, "Fuck – Steve! I've just stepped in dog shit!"

Seamus shook his wizened head, but did not allow the lack of symbolic menace to discourage him. Something arcane and disturbing was about to happen, he was sure of it.

He eased the book out from its tower of tomes and drank in the gold-engraved title: "Sex Magick – The Real Thing and None of That Fake Bollocks". Beneath these words, a symbol had not been drawn but *carved* into the cover: a teardrop shape with an "X" cut through its bulging base. Seamus had seen the mark once before, many decades ago, during the doomed afternoon that had laid the path he had pursued for the rest of his life.

He listened for the thunderbolt again, hearing only the rustling of the teen's game of pocket snooker.

DEMON THINGY

The pages of the book were yellow, fragile. They contained no printed words, but sentences had been scrawled in badly-spelled block capitals. Doodles described rituals and rites, sacrifices and sex acts, as well as, for some reason, a recipe for peanut butter brownies. Towards the end of the book, Seamus discovered the true reason he had been drawn to it.

His stomach tightened.

"Hello again," he purred.

He stroked the page.

A childish pencil diagram depicted the front and rear of a grey creature with ragged wings and a single yellow horn protruding from its skull. Upon its back was the teardrop-and-"X" design, dripping with scribbled blood.

This was a mark that Seamus himself had once inflicted upon the very living, breathing, horrifying beast that the image represented.

He gazed, mesmerised.

Although there was still no thunder to be heard, outside, the grey clouds started to spit.

DEMON THINGY

3

"It hurts today, brother," Alexander said, his frail, naked limbs spread across the Airbnb apartment's mattress.

The room smelled rotten, like dead foliage, as it always did on Gustav's brother's bad days.

Edward sat on the floor in the corner, reading Shevchenko's poetry by the glow of a clip-on book-light. He checked his nails and polished them on his shirt. There was still something miraculous about Gustav's abilities, but it was strange how, in such a short while, Edward had accepted them as truth.

Magic was real; Edward had seen it. He had *experienced* it.

Gustav stood beside his brother Alexander, a rotund, sturdy-looking figure hovering above what appeared to be a shrivelled corpse. They had the same fiercely intense brown eyes and similarly

Slavic cheekbones, but while Gustav's extra weight gave him an almost friendly appearance, Alexander's gaunt cheeks and deep eye sockets made him appear faintly threatening most of the time. Today, though, he appeared exactly as he was: terribly ill.

"We mustn't leave it so long, next time," Gustav said. "I know we were travelling, but still..."

Alexander's words were sighs. "We do what must be done. As it always has been."

"Yes brother," Gustav replied. "But we must always find time to refresh you."

"Just do it now, Gustav. Our flames only burn for so long." Alexander coughed, and for a moment, when Edward glanced up from his book again, it was as though he could see through the flesh of Alexander's brother's cheeks, as if the sickness was wearing away his substance and turning him translucent.

Gustav straightened up and raised his hands. "In the name of the Father, the Son, and the Holy Ghost, I command you: *desist*."

DEMON THINGY

Edward looked up yet again. It may have been blasphemy to have said so, but he suspected that Gustav's powers came, not from anything holy, but from his own colourful history. Whatever it was, though, it sure as hell worked, and that was a blessing in itself.

Gustav lowered his pudgy hands, so that they were just an inch or two from his brother Alexander's pasty flesh.

"Desist, disease. Halt your progress. Crawl back into the nothingness from whence you came."

Edward sighed. These Ukrainian siblings spoke gooder English than what he did.

"*DESIST!*" Gustav cried suddenly, and at his words there was a hissing snap, like a snake being whacked with a spatula.

In the very same instant, Alexander's flesh coloured, his eyes whitened, and his frail arms and legs seemed to inflate. It was not air that filled them, though: it was muscle, firm and healthy, and it gave Alexander's cadaverous form a fresh burst of vigour. His sunken stomach rose and became chiselled, his hair gained sheen, and his pinched lips puffed out to reclaim some of their charm. Edward couldn't avoid noticing that even Alexander's limp penis twitched and thickened in response to his brother's words.

"We are here to vanquish the darkness, and to spread the word of truth," Gustav said.

"Amen," Edward and the newly revived Alexander said.

"We are charged to rid the world of evil," Gustav said.

"Amen!" Edward said again.

"We are the Children of Chernobyl," Gustav said.

"*AMEN!*"

Alexander sat up straight and smiled.

Gustav collapsed.

DEMON THINGY

4

It wasn't as though Clark enjoyed screwing people over, but when the cupboard of his and Jackoby's temporary room was barer than a grizzly, it was time for some pube-deep screwing.

The old couple's doorbell rang a couple of bars from the Monty Python theme tune. Clark's lanky, gawky colleague Jackoby – dressed in fluorescent orange safety gear, unshaven for days and unwashed for longer – made a fart noise after the doorbell had stopped, and giggled. Black and yellow teeth appeared between his lips, and his skinny face lit up with joy. Clark once more reflected that his loyal colleague really did look like a tall, humanoid ferret on its hind legs.

They waited outside the semi-detached patiently, knowing that the wrinkly pair who they'd happened to see shuffling into the house a couple of days ago weren't the quickest of movers.

DEMON THINGY

As was Clark and Jackoby's way, they were only passing through this cruddy little West Midlands town of Walsall, because it usually took less than a month for someone to decide to kick their heads in. So far, they'd kept their un-kicked heads low, and the only crime they'd committed since arriving was selling a gram of terrible weed to an ancient, drunken pensioner they'd met at a pub.

They didn't specifically target old fogies; it had just happened that way.

They heard a lady call out from inside the house. Probably Mrs Roberts, if the online phone directory was right.

Clark winked at Jackoby, straightening his wonky tie, holding up a clipboard and ignoring the familiar sense of guilt that tightened his throat. He hoped that his unmistakable air of sophistication would make up for Jackoby's oafish idiocy. He pinched one nostril, blew a grape-sized booger out of the other, and said, "Remember: you need the toilet."

DEMON THINGY

"Yup," Jackoby nodded, smoothing down the vibrant builder's overalls he'd nabbed from an active site near the canal. "Good gear, this. Reckon I could get a few quid for it."

There was a rattle of locks. Clark beamed a smile.

When the door opened a crack, a small, white-haired lady peered out over half-moon spectacles. "Yes?"

"Mrs Delia Roberts," Clark greeted, holding out an unlaminated fake ID he'd printed off at the library.

The old woman squinted. "Yes?"

Clark said, "We are here on behalf of Friedrich Building Contractors Limited." He held up his clipboard to silence her protests. "I am fully aware that you have not been expecting us, and that you have had no prior engagement with myself or my colleague here..."

"Ello," Jackoby said.

"...or in fact, our company."

DEMON THINGY

"No, no I haven't," Mrs Roberts said, and opened the door a little wider. She wore a long grey dress, a plum-coloured cardigan, and a metal pendant around her neck that looked like a banana. She was wringing her hands, either due to nerves or because they were hurting for some reason. Her eyes were narrow, which gave her a look of befuddlement.

"We are here on council business, Mrs Roberts," said Clark. "I don't mean to worry you, but there has recently been some urgent talk about land subsidence on this street. Something about the old mines under the road?"

"Ooh," she said. "Oh dear."

Clark continued, "Now, we *could* go through the usual bureaucratic processes and notify our superiors, get them to authorise a visit, send you a letter, etc, etc..."

"Oh, yes," she said, continuing to look bewildered.

"Or." Clark paused. "I suppose we could have a little look-see now and see if we can't sort the problem a little quicker?"

DEMON THINGY

"Well..." she said.

"To be honest, it will be better for us to go for our lunch breaks now and come and see you in a month or two, but the problem is only going to get worse the longer we leave it."

"Right," she said, looking fretful. "Well, I suppose you had better come in then. It won't take long, will it?"

"No, of course not," Clark said.

The old woman opened the door wide. Clark and Jackoby stepped into a hallway lined with framed swirling patterns of red and blue. The carpet smelled dusty.

Once the door was shut, Clark nodded to Jackoby and coughed.

"Oh yeah," he muttered. "Can I use your bathroom?"

"Um," the woman said. She looked apprehensive, continuing to wring her hands, but said, "Yes, of course. Upstairs, second door on the left."

"Thanks," Jackoby smiled, winked at Clark without the slightest degree of subtlety and mounted the beige carpeted steps.

"Now, Mrs Roberts," Clark said, keen to distract her. "Will you show me the kitchen, please? Let's get this little issue sorted."

"Ooh, yes dear, of course," the old lady said.

Mrs Roberts shuffled along the hallway in front of Clark, the bun of white hair atop her head just level with his chin. A gold, gem-studded hairpin penetrated the bun. Clark wondered if he could slip it from her hair without her noticing.

While his irritating friend and colleague was no doubt hunting upstairs for money and valuables, Clark wet a finger, turned a page on his clipboard and began the arduous task of pulling the wool over yet another poor sap's eyes. He opened his mouth to begin his spiel, but before he could continue there was a crash from upstairs.

What the hell had that clumsy prat broken now?

DEMON THINGY

"Oooh, whatever can that be?" Mrs Roberts asked. But she was smiling a smile so bright that her teeth could only have been falsies.

"Jackoby!" Clark called. "What did you do?"

Mrs Roberts' smile seemed to widen further. She no longer looked uncertain of anything at all. In fact, she looked *predatory*.

There was a moan from the hallway and a stagger of feet on the steps. Clark pushed past the old bag into the corridor and was confronted by a gut-chundering smell and a man whose head was smeared brown-and-red, his eyes hidden by a thick, lumpy mess.

Jackoby was groaning. In one hand, he held a clump of banknotes. In the other, a fistful of jewellery.

A bald, stocky old man with a bristly moustache loomed at the top of the stairs, holding an antique chamber-pot. He had a similar expression to that of the old lady, but Clark liked his even less.

DEMON THINGY

Clark went to dash for the front door, but when he felt something dig into his throat his legs collapsed beneath him. He dropped to his knees and withdrew the hairpin from the side of his neck, staring in disbelief at the glittering gems as his torso became completely numb. He flopped forwards, his nose popping on the carpet, and used his legs to roll onto his side.

From behind, the old man shoved Jackoby down the stairs, whose face was a mask of blood and, judging by the whiff, thick dollops of shit. The back of his head landed directly before Clark's eyes.

Mr Roberts descended the stairs, fiddling with his flies.

"Come on now, Horace," Mrs Roberts said, out of Clark's line of sight. "Mind your heart."

Clark whimpered, but he'd lost all control of his body and Jackoby must have been out cold.

"It's alright, love. I'm not going to fuck 'em," the old man said. Just before he reached the bottom of the steps, he withdrew a decrepit wang from his zipper. "I think I'm just going to cum on them."

The last Clark heard, before he fell mercifully unconscious, was a tut, and Mrs Roberts saying, "Righty-ho, I'll pop the kettle on, then."

DEMON THINGY

5

Seamus's house was an arcane treasure trove of the bizarre. Animal skulls sat upon the shelves, hung from the walls, and were used as ashtrays for Seamus's pipe. Ornaments forged by wizards, sorceresses and witch doctors crammed Seamus's coffee table; mainly likenesses of men with cartoonish members or women with over-exaggerated breasts and buttocks. There were swords, which 99%-rated Ebay members claimed had slain demons and spectres; there were wands once wielded by warlocks and wise-women from centuries past; and there were books – oh, the books! Heaps, towers, and occasional monoliths of paper and card stood from floor to ceiling in every room, detailing the intricate "ins and outs" of magick in all its glorious forms.

Despite having dedicated his life to esotericism, Seamus had experienced few benefits as a result. He was poor, and had never been rich.

DEMON THINGY

He was single, and always had been. Even worse, he possessed no way of consummating a carnal cuddle, due to having lost his means of doing so as a confused teen.

Seamus estimated that 99.427% of all witchery and wizardry was drivelous nonsense. That was why, segregated from the publications that he had confirmed as codswallop, Seamus had a very special chamber containing the 0.573% of writings with which he had attained success.

With one book, "Professor Merkin's Thelemic Ceremonies of Transmogrification", Seamus had trapped a bumble bee in a jam-jar and turned it into a butterfly. The pretty little bug, which had survived in its glass cage for five full days following its transformation, had wings that each bore a detailed depiction of a human breast. The butterfly, now dead for many decades, remained in its jar, perched atop the very book that had once altered its state from a stinger into a flutterer.

Using another guide, "Remedies for Maladies using Melodies and Threnodies", Seamus had revived a roadkilled fox he had peeled up from the tarmac. Having painstakingly translated the book's text from ancient Sumerian into English, Seamus had sung its words in a variety of different styles to the squashed animal, until it had blinked twice, and, despite its snapped spine, licked the oozing knots of its spilled intestines. Then it had flopped back to Sleepyland, forever.

Seamus hadn't wanted a life of mumbo-jumbo and fruitless purchases. Until one fateful day, he had been quite intent on marrying a good woman and having her pop out 2.4 children. That dream had died shortly after Seamus's friend, Jimbo McGarth, had said, "Hey, do you fancy trying something a bit different?"

As a curious adolescent stoner during the 60s, Seamus was all about trying new things. None of the local mop-topped hippies had managed to come through with the acid tabs they'd kept promising, but Seamus had enjoyed quite a number of alternative hallucinogens. He was also head-over-heels in love with Maureen Conway, a blonde, blue-eyed, flower-skirt-wearing, lush-lipped and tight-bottomed barmaid. When Jimbo had explained that he wanted to try out a spellbook he had stolen from his grandmother's attic, Seamus's first thought was to use it as an opportunity to seduce young Maureen, who he knew had an interest in spiritualism.

It no longer pained Seamus to picture all that had happened afterwards; in many ways, it had given his life a purpose. But while that day had given him a path to follow, it had robbed him of his manhood and the opportunity of porking young Maureen, or any other pretty thing he may have successfully sweet-talked. The loss of that chance, as well as Seamus's rather unique digestive system, had left him feeling terribly wronged, and knowing that one day he would be due recompense.

There was a chance that this fabled day had arrived.

6

Seamus sat nude on the green rock floor, the cavern where his penis should have been glistening in the low light. His buttocks were mashed into a cushion to avoid the onset of further haemorrhoids, and he was trying to keep calm. He stroked his long grey beard in apprehension.

The room he was in, which looked like the inside of a dark beach cave, should not have existed. However, thanks to one of the five-or-so spells that Seamus had mastered he'd been able to gouge a hole in the fabric of reality to perform his upcoming mystical ritual. While he should have been nervous at the prospect of summoning an eldritch entity, he was almost as concerned about hauling his ancient frame back to his feet.

Seamus sighed. It was a sick joke that in order to summon the beast who had deprived him of his dong, Seamus required the use of one.

DEMON THINGY

Luckily, with a neighbour like Seamus's, he'd had no guilt in borrowing a donor.

His next-door-neighbour, Gilbert O'Bandaharrrrrgh, had told Seamus to keep his ritualistic chanting down one too many times. Now he lay unconscious and undressed on the ground a few feet away, gagged with a sock and parcel tape, hands taped together and resting on his furry belly. Even Gilbert's dinky little three-incher made Seamus's stomach acid boil with jealous rage. How *dare* a scruffy little blowhard like Gilbert possess such a magnificent tube of meat, such an instrument of slime-squirting joy, and yet Seamus had been forced to live bereft for so long?

Between them, Seamus had lain out a rough circle of bread dough, dotted with hamster eyeballs. Inside this strange ring, Seamus had erected a tripod of three legs that bore a single, three-foot-tall protrusion, pointing towards the ceiling. Scattered at its feet, Seamus had splashed some blood drawn from a slash in his now-bandaged left ankle, scattered 12 lukewarm roast potatoes, and sprinkled the sex juices of a disabled female swan, crippled and frigged raw by Seamus himself earlier that day. All he needed now was the hot ejaculate of a living human male – something that Seamus was unable to naturally provide.

Seamus took a roast potato and pushed it up his arse. It needed more rosemary, but wasn't bad.

"Come on then – let's get this over with," he said, tugging on a pair of yellow marigold gloves.

Seamus held up the crumpled A4 sheet upon which he had scrawled the translated incantation, and began to read. "I call upon Azimuth: chainer of mutant shrimps, wielder of spatulas, scourge of moderately endowed estate agents – hear me!" The shout woke Gilbert from his daze, and the poor naked chap blinked sleepily. "I also call upon Brazclath: caresser of eels, fellater of trombones, fighter of rabid sloths – hear me! And finally, to complete this blasphemous triangle, I call upon ... Graham! You, who once bathed in the menstrual gore of the hermaphrodite scoutmasters of Thebes, who vanquished the arse-bollocked minotaur of

Saturn, and who decapitated the thousand-headed gimp-hydra of Scunthorpe...hear me!"

The light, which had no clear source, flickered.

"Azimuth, Brazclath and Graham – I offer you these...offerings!" Seamus declared. "Potatoes, roasted in the fat of a grieving mallard, representing the sustenance I am willing to sacrifice to gather your attention. The vadge-slop of a swan, symbolising a blessing of fertility, grace and beauty. My own blood, proving my vital dedication to this act. Three dozen hamster eyes poked into a circle of bread dough, because...um...actually, I forget. But now, the final ingredient: the very substance I crave to produce myself: human spunk!"

Now came the hard part: getting up. With a howl like a constipated hyena, Seamus heaved himself to his feet. His captive neighbour had until then remained silent, but as Seamus hobbled towards him, careful not to disrupt the circle, Gilbert O'Bandaharrrrrgh mewled through the sock in protest.

DEMON THINGY

"Oh do pipe down," Seamus said. "I'm only going to toss you off and then feed you a forgetfulness potion, so you've got nothing to whine about."

Seamus sat down beside Gilbert with a pained grunt and took the man's member between his fingers. Having been penis-free since his teens, Seamus was no expert in the art of masturbation; however, it took just seconds to have Gilbert standing to attention.

"Now, Azimuth, Brazclath, and Graham," Seamus said, jerking Gilbert's winky. "I beg of you – accept these oblations and drag the Nameless One to me!"

The light flashed like a strobe. A gust of wind whistled through the cave-like chamber.

"Come, cacodaemons!" Seamus yelled. "Come, magickal imps! Come black angels, dark demigods and triple-nippled ghouls! Drag the Nameless One, shrieking and shitting, to this earthly realm!"

DEMON THINGY

Gilbert moaned. It was impossible to tell whether he was protesting or starting to enjoy himself.

Seamus heard a rising noise, like a distant aeroplane scorching the heavens. Seamus kept wanking. Gilbert kept grunting. The lights kept extinguishing and un-stinguishing. Rain pattered the stony roof above them and, in the circle of bread dough and rodent eyeballs, the dim outline of something waist-high began to materialise.

Gilbert squealed and popped his cork, spurting white ribbons into the air. Although Seamus was suddenly terrified, he felt a burst of triumph as he batted the stolen sperm from the air and into the circle. Wherever a droplet landed, there was a hiss and a jet of steam.

Blackness devoured the cave-room.

Surprising himself with his energy, Seamus scampered back from the circle. He heard Gilbert grunt once more in the dark, followed by the harsh breathing of ... something else. Seamus pressed his spine against the cold rock wall, wishing he could put more space between himself and the new occupant.

Seamus held his breath and listened to what seemed like the gusting nostrils of a mad bull. Gilbert had fallen silent too, perhaps even more petrified than Seamus, given how little he probably understood about what was happening. To Seamus, he had successfully summoned his life-long nemesis; to Gilbert, he'd been kidnapped, tied up and wanked off, as part of a supernatural ritual.

The furious breathing slowed, and two crimson spheres appeared in the gloom. Gilbert whimpered. A heavy footstep stomped the hard floor. There was another suggestion of movement, then a *whoompf* and a vibrant flash of orange. The Nameless One roared, and in that burst of light Seamus witnessed its form, anally impaled by the steel tripod.

The bipedal frame was just as he remembered: wizened, hairless, grey, and so thin as to be almost skeletal. Hunched, The Nameless One's ribs protruded and its gnarled hands flexed at its sides. Wings extended from its spine, like a

DEMON THINGY

bat's, but without the finger-like muscles extending to their tips. Lit by the burst of flame, it was the sight of the thing's face that would soon fill Seamus's nightmares: a crusted horn growing from its creased forehead, an impossibly elongated jaw, a snout much like a warthog's, and eye sockets that bore no organs of sight, only burning craters that glowed redder than blood. And on its back, out of sight from Seamus, Seamus knew that there was the tear-and-X symbol which he had inflicted upon it, 59 long years ago.

The light vanished once more.

A voice that Seamus had once heard, way back in the early days of his life – a scratching, slithering, scrape of a voice – said, "*You...*"

Ignoring his terror, Seamus replied, "Yep, it's me, you old tosser. Pleased to see me?"

The red balls swept the gloom. "*You are ungrateful, old man,*" it continued. "*You should be licking my feet in appreciation.*"

Seamus scoffed in the dark. "And why would I do that?"

DEMON THINGY

"Because when you were young I only stole your manhood. I could have taken your head."

"It might have been better if you had," Seamus said, feeling bitter. "You left me dickless and forced me to eat through my own arse, you bastard! Every day, I've lived like that! Every day, for the 59 pathetic bloody years since!"

The Nameless One chuckled stickily; perhaps the worst sound that Seamus had ever heard. *"And so you have called me again, trapped me in a puny snare, in the hope that if you plead and grovel enough I'll return you to your former state."*

Despite its power, omniscience was clearly not one of its traits. "No," Seamus said.

"No?" it asked. *"Then what?"*

Unexpectedly, Seamus's fear momentarily evaporated. "I wouldn't beg for your help if I was being gang-buggered by radioactive gorillas."

There was a whistling, irritated sigh.

"I know what I have to do," Seamus said. "If I keep you trapped long enough, I won't have to beg."

The sigh became a mucoid huff, as of something much larger than the slim grey form that Seamus had seen in the flame-burst.

"66 days and six hours," Seamus gloated. "That's how long you're going to be here for. After that, you'll have to do *everything* I say."

"Even the ignorant know that the number '666' is a mistranslated myth."

"We'll see," Seamus said.

At his words, the cave-room flooded with that fiery light again, and the Nameless One, snarling, stretched one arm out over the protective circle. As the diminutive beast reached for Seamus with a ragged talon, the entire space within the ring of bread dough was engulfed by flames. Seamus was beyond its reach, but Gilbert was not. Although Seamus could see nothing of its form through the inferno, the skinny grey arm dove down and snatched at Gilbert's ankle. The Nameless One did not dare to step outside of the circle but, snorting and bellowing, it hauled on Gilbert's leg like a child trying to pull free a thin tree branch. Gilbert's cries were muffled by the

DEMON THINGY

sock and by the Nameless One's roars, even as his entire leg was wrenched free from its socket. Gilbert's eyes were vast plates in the last moments of dwindling fire-light, and the space where his leg had been only moments before gouted blood in spits and spurts. The leg's amputater held it aloft like a joint of meat, and as it returned its arm to the circle, the flames retracted and ceased, and darkness fell again.

Seamus whinnied in terror and dragged himself to his feet. He slid along the rocky wall towards where he knew the stairs were, bracing himself against gristly snaps and wet crunches that he wished he couldn't hear.

"You won't last 66 days, you ancient fool," Seamus heard, as he descended the lightless steps back to his home.

"We'll see," Seamus repeated, hearing the tremble in his tone.

At least he wouldn't be needing that Forgetfulness potion anymore.

DEMON THINGY

7

To claim that Pie-Eyed was a typical bakery would be both true and false; 99% of its clientele were pastry-purchasing pedestrians who would never witness the clandestine meetings that took place beneath the shop floor.

Mr and Mrs Roberts waited patiently in line, large and bald Mr Roberts in his ubiquitous tweed suit and clutching a bag-for-life, and Mrs Roberts in a fetching black chemise, her usual white bob propped up beside a hairband bearing a small top hat leant jauntily.

Mrs Roberts had awoken feeling unsettled following her encounter with the Great Old Horny One, and those two pillocks who'd tried to rob them that morning had done nothing to improve her mood. Even worse, her bloody arthritis was giving her jip again, making her hands feel taut and achey.

DEMON THINGY

That blue-and-bushy-haired harlot Beverly was serving behind the counter at Pie-Eyed that day, pinching her lips whenever a customer spoke as if she was chewing a peeled lime. As the conga line of those eager for hot sustenance shortened, Mrs Roberts eyed the scones, doughnuts and eclairs, knowing full well they'd play havoc with her diabetes. She applied a smile. "Good morning, Beverly. How are you today?"

Beverly pinched her lips and narrowed her eyes, their crow's feet wrinkling. "What can I do *you* for?"

Mrs Roberts scratched her chin in thought. "Can I have a brown loaf and four sausage rolls please?"

Beverly "hmphed", and then whizzed about bagging their order. Mrs Roberts knew that Beverly had always been jealous of her superior cheekbones, as well as the way she could pop out her teeth whenever she wanted. She also suspected that the blue-tinged slapper was annoyed at it being her turn to run the tills and hold fort up in the bakery, when such an important event was about to take place downstairs.

Mrs Roberts handed over the money and asked, "Can we use the second disabled toilet, please?"

Beverly pinged open the till and passed Mrs Roberts her change with a mumbled, "Of course." Then she reached beneath the counter.

"Your hair looks lovely today, dear," Mrs Roberts said to the shock-haired till operator as they passed. "It's enough to make a sea anemone jealous."

The door at the end of the shop, the second disabled toilet, bore a permanent "Out of Order" sign. Before they opened it, the Robertses glanced back at the diminishing queue and spied a tall, ominous figure in a hooded black robe coming in. The figure was skinny enough to make the Grim Reaper feel like he needed to lose a few pounds, and its face was lost to the shadows of its hood. It carried a plastic bag, full of something wet and red.

DEMON THINGY

A few customers rolled their eyes at this person who, it appeared to them, was wearing fancy dress on an early Monday afternoon.

The tall figure waved cheerily to the Robertses by the door. In a high-pitched, nasal voice, it called, "Coo-ee! Mr and Mrs Roberts! I'm here for the big day!"

Mrs Roberts, mortified, pushed open the disabled toilet door and hurried inside. "Come *on*, Horace!" she urged her husband, turning back and seeing him grinning like a dolt.

Clive, the moron who as usual had turned up in his robes rather than bringing them along in a bag like any normal, self-respecting Satan worshipper, followed them through the disabled toilet door. It led, not into what Mrs Roberts thought of as a "cripplebog", but an elevator.

"Hello, Clive," Mrs Roberts said, as the giant figure stepped inside.

Clive pulled the hood down and revealed a chiselled face. His frame and behaviour gave the impression that someone had used one of those magic cinema tickets from that amusing Arnold

DEMON THINGY

Schwarzenegger film to yank Frank Spencer out of his sitcom, stretched him on a rack, and forced him to dress like the Death; however, he was in fact a rather fetching young man. Pity that he had to be as queer as a four-headed vibrator. "Nice morning for it, eh?" he said, scratching one sweaty cheek before lifting his hood again.

"Definitely," Mr Roberts said from the corner of the lift, pulling his own robes out of his bag-for-life. There was something earthy in his tone.

Mrs Roberts shivered. There had been a time when her husband had hungered for her, but these days he stared at Clive in the same manner he had stared at her when they'd first met. And if she was honest with herself, her husband had always gotten more from prodding at her balloon knot than from taking a ride in her pink canoe. Lucky that she had the Old Horny Beast to look after her every now and again, because without him she'd have been doomed to rely on satisfaction from The Stallion, her favourite rubber companion.

DEMON THINGY

Mrs Roberts brushed a few white hairs off Mr Roberts' black robes, wishing she had brought her lint roller. The other acolytes made such an effort for the meetings; she even suspected that some of them dyed their robes.

The lift door drew open and their hooded leader approached them with a swish of vivid red fabric. Balloon-headed, moon-bellied Lady Saffron Baker was the self-appointed head of the coven, and reputedly the last in a line of witches who had for centuries owned the property and its special apartment beneath the basement. Lady Saffron often claimed that the blood of a Sfenigh, the offspring of a demon and witch, ran through her veins, and gave her magical powers. Mrs Roberts could not deny having witnessed her abilities, but while Lady Saffron was *technically* capable of performing intricate rites and ceremonies, her unfortunate speech impediment often threw a spanner in the works.

"Mr Woberts," Lady Saffron greeted. "Mrs Woberts." She turned her head. "Cwive."

"No, Clive," the camp, cowled spectre said.

DEMON THINGY

"Yes," Mrs Saffron agreed, and turned back to the assembled throng of hooded figures. "Our number is compwete!" she announced. "We begin in 5 minutes. Anyone who needs a wee should go now."

The coven room was lit with six hundred and sixty-six red candles – Ikea had a sale on – and the walls were painted black with occult symbols and some *lovely* fucsia trim. An alter stood at the far end before the group of 20 or so members, the number of which dipped or rose depending on the doddery congregation's ailing health, or whether a meeting coincided with any gripping ITV dramas. That was why today's important gathering had been arranged for the morning; so that no one could use a Silent Witness rerun as an excuse not to turn up.

Clive and Mr Roberts followed Mrs Roberts as she pushed her way to the front of the group, who were taking advantage of the opportunity to natter, bicker and complain before the ritual began. They all appeared like a posse of Halloween-goers, who had dressed in theme. Only Dave, who was even taller than Clive and as broad as a bull, stood out from the black-cloaked crowd.

Lady Saffron stood before the altar, with a dark, waist-high cauldron at her feet. Her robes were the colour of blood, as she was the only member permitted to wear anything other than black. Mrs Roberts thought that black would have been a better colour for her weight, but had never said anything. "Awise, members of the Baker's Coven."

We're already bloody standing, you imbecile, Mrs Roberts thought.

The other hooded members shuffled their feet awkwardly. Somebody farted. Lady Saffron's robed head darted in the sound's direction. One or two stifled sniggers broke free, but died when Lady Saffron stamped her foot and bellowed, "Siwence!" Then: "Bwing me the ingwedients."

Five acolytes, including Clive, stepped out from the congregation and lined up before the cauldron. The first held out a simple urn.

"The ashes of a paedophiwic pwiest," Mrs Roberts intoned. She reached out and allowed the acolyte to pour the holy man's cremated remains into her hands. "*Hail Satan!*"

The congregation replied, "*HAIL SATAN!*"

Mrs Roberts smiled in reminiscence – ah yes, Father Sweeney. He had been a pleasant man really, for a servant of God. She had once lifted her petticoat for him after a night of drunken abandon down the pub. Father Sweeney had been quite thorough when she had commanded him to nibble, suckle and delve into her sodden folds; a surprisingly cunning linguist, for a priest.

It had almost been a shame to have driven him to suicide, but there was no way that any other denizen of the Baker's Coven could have organised such an ingredient for the ritual. While Lady Saffron admittedly had a smattering of occult knowledge and a sprinkling of unholy powers, it was always Mrs Roberts who arranged for anything complicated or challenging. Without her, she thought, the Baker's Coven would have been no more than a coffee morning with silly outfits and a couple of magic tricks.

DEMON THINGY

Lady Saffron sprinkled Father Sweeney's powdery remnants into the black pot, and then nodded to Clive, who was next in line.

"Now," he said, from the blackness of his hood. "I wasn't sure quite what you meant when you asked me to get a 'black cock', so I covered both bases."

Lady Saffron huffed. "A male chicken. A wooster."

"Well, it's your choice." Clive plucked a farm bird from the plastic bag and shook it awake. It clucked, sounding baffled. "Had to bop it on the head a few times, so it's prob'ly a bit out of sorts!"

Lady Saffron took it by the throat and drew a golden dagger from her robe.

"Anyone want this?" Clive asked, holding up a sad-looking severed organ.

It was nothing to write home about, but Mrs Roberts felt sure that if it was filled with a little fluid and she added a tourniquet… "I'll, um, *dispose* of that."

DEMON THINGY

As Mrs Roberts slipped the detached penis into an inside pocket, Lady Saffron went at the confused cockerel like a Weightwatchers warrior princess. Feathers puffed about and viscous gore squirted the alter. When the beast was slain she dropped it into the pot. Lady Saffron nodded to the remaining three coven members, who, facing away from the congregation, then lifted their robes to reveal three scrawny, pale bottoms.

"Now," Lady Saffron boomed. "Bind our spell with your seed!"

The trio began frantically masturbating. Two of them went off like water pistols, firing long white spurts into the cauldron before shuffling back into the audience. The third was clearly struggling.

There were a couple of titters.

"Just give me a moment, will you?" he mumbled, using a thumb and forefinger to try and yank his wee willy winky into submission.

The congregation, easily distracted, began to gossip.

DEMON THINGY

Mrs Roberts stepped forwards. "May I?"

The embarrassed tosser turned and nodded his hood.

Instead of jerking his gherkin though, Mrs Roberts slipped her middle finger between his pimpled bumcheeks.

"Ooh," the acolyte said.

Mrs Roberts found his prostate and he let out a colossal groan, spraying the cauldron with cock-snot. "Thanks," he said to his saviour, and waddled off as if he'd been kicked in the bollocks.

"The incantation begins!" Lady Saffron thundered. She tugged her crimson hood back to reveal her round face. "On your knees in pwepewation!"

There was a chorus of moans and groans and cracks of backs as the coven members struggled down to their clapped-out knees.

Lady Saffron fumbled inside her robes and fished out a pair of large-lensed spectacles. She then held a neon post-it note close to her face and began to chant – or at least tried to. "Pess ...

DEMON THINGY

pesspetui te ... um ... domine ... er ... I think that says 'arsehole'..."

She showed the pink slip to a nearby coven member who shook their head.

"Yes, it's all Latin to me," Lady Saffron said. She sniggered at her own joke.

Anger filled Mrs Roberts. The summoning ceremony was becoming the mockery she had always known it would. Lady Saffron couldn't have summoned an obedient dog.

"PESSPETUI TE ARSEHOLE! I think that's wight. ACCESSO OBSCUWISSIMI SUNT ABYSSI!"

The coven tried hard to repeat the incantation, but it was almost impossible to decipher her lisp-addled rant.

Mrs Roberts remembered the words of the Great Horny One, demanding that she claim the coven in his name. She certainly intended to usurp that witless twerp Lady Saffron, but now was not the time. Mrs Roberts believed, however, that if she allowed Lady Saffron to screw up yet another demonic summoning, then the congregation may just become more bendable to Mrs Roberts' will.

The coven would become hers, and Mrs Roberts' rightful place in hell would be hers, too.

"PISSPOTTY ARSEHOLE!" the acolytes yelled. "ACCESSO OBSCURISSIMI STUNTA RICH TEA!"

"IMPEWATA FACERE ET WESURGES GEHENNAM IGNIS!" Lady Saffron shouted. "EX-PATCHOULI ... oh, where's the other bit of paper?"

"IMPERATA FACERE ET RESURGES GEHENNAM IGNIS!" the congregation bellowed, in the correct pronunciation.

And the cauldron began to tremble.

Mrs Roberts tutted.

To her disappointment, something was actually happening.

8

Their mother had told Alexander Dudyk, and Alexander had told his brother Gustav, that in the 3rd trimester of her pregnancy with Gustav, on April 26th, 1986, in the dark hours of the early morning, explosions had rocked the city of Pripyat, Chernobyl. Mummy Dudyk had awoken clutching her belly, gripped by a certainty that everything in her life was about to change.

By 6am, their mother had been vomiting far more violently than morning sickness usually caused: aggressive coughing, the taste of iron on her tongue, and wave after wave of shivering pain. Their father, who Gustav had no memory of, had insisted that they visit the hospital, but their mother's sickness had faded by midday. Their mother had once told Alexander that she had felt something throbbing inside her, as if energy thrummed had from her unborn baby's soul, healing her, or at least holding the symptoms of the radiation at bay.

Although the city of Pripyat had continued as normal the following day, only dimly aware of the power plant fire that had burst forth and been extinguished during the blackest hours of the night, another day later the evacuation broadcast had invaded the homes of the residents. Gustav and Alexander's mother had listened to the broadcast, absorbed the calm words of the announcer as she'd described the radiation and the deteriorating local conditions, and that healing throb had emanated from Gustav in her womb once again. With that warm flow of energy, she had realised the gift she had been blessed with: Gustav must have been touched by God Himself. He was a blessing – perhaps the only true blessing that life had bestowed on her so far – but this stage of her pregnancy was a fragile time for the unborn child. If she were to move away from their home now, how could she know that she wouldn't ruin whatever holy gifts her son would one day bring to the world?

DEMON THINGY

When the police-escorted buses began to ferry families away from the evacuation area, the family of three, plus bump, watched from the roof of their apartment block with enough supplies to last a few days. Together, they had watched from above as the city had been emptied, residents taking only the most basic of supplies and leaving their cars abandoned, their homes locked and shuttered against what would prove to be a very long night.

Gustav and Alexander's father had been the only one of the family to succumb almost immediately to the radiation. Although Mummy Dudyk's symptoms had retracted with each warm pulse of Gustav's foetus, Daddy Dudyk had collapsed two days later, vomited blood in four, and died within a week of returning to their home.

Mummy Dudyk had told Alexander that it was because of his father's lack of belief. She knew that her unborn child was a blessing from the father of creation, and if Daddy Dudyk had died so quickly, it could only mean that he had not been pious enough to bear the weight of raising such a momentous baby.

They had dragged Daddy Dudyk's oozing corpse to the window at the end of the corridor outside their apartment. A skip lay five floors below, so they had dropped Daddy Dudyk through the window and burned his body in the empty forecourt of their apartment block, at the centre of the ghost-city that their home of Pripyat had become.

Baby Gustav kept kicking, while Alexander and Mummy Dudyk remained in good health. They looted the silent homes nearby, taking only what they had needed, and Mummy Dudyk taught Alexander more of her strict religious ways. She was to give birth to an angel, she had said, and in a world where nuclear power plants could end lives and ravage bodies with agonizing sickness, an angel would have plenty of work to do.

Gustav was born four weeks overdue, in their home bath: a large, plump, rose-pink, normal-looking child, and Alexander had told Gustav that he had loved him from the moment he had dragged the Gustav from his mother's body. With no one else to love or care for during the five years they had survived alone in Pripyat, they had foraged, played, and prayed together during every waking moment. The family of three had lived in isolation, and during constant sermons, Mummy Dudyk had praised her growing son's ability to keep them safe and healthy in a radioactive home that would have proven deadly to anyone else – anyone without a blessed cherub to protect them, that was. Eventually, that unbalanced certainty had led Mummy Dudyk to declare that it was time to leave Pripyat, and venture out into the world to find her perfect, angelic child's true calling.

And in a roundabout, twisty-turny way, that had brought Gustav and his brother Alexander to the van in which they now waited.

It was a fair-sized vehicle. Its rear, where the fat and skinny pair of brothers now sat, was windowless but lit by a battery-charged strip-lamp attached to the ceiling. There were no chairs, so they were forced to sit on the ground cross-legged. It was also rather musty, but having

DEMON THINGY

started their lives in a post-nuclear wasteland and having frequently moved from home to home ever since, the brothers were unfazed by dust or grime. What they *were* concerned with, though, was piety and faith. This was why, above a dirt-smudged floor scattered with discarded food containers, all kinds of Christian symbols and relics were reverently arranged. The carved wooden crucifix that had hung above their childhood fireplace now gazed down over them from a position above the rear doors, while beneath it were replica paintings of St Paul, St Barnabus, and St Colostomus the Dreary. There was also a mini-altar screwed to one side of the van interior, a bookcase containing several religious texts including a bible penned by Reverend Cliff Richard himself (peace be upon him), and a cabinet containing four Evian bottles' worth of blessed water.

"What ... what *is* that?" Gustav asked, a sandwich paused midway to his mouth. A slice of greasy salami slid from the dry bread and stuck to his rotund belly, turning his plain white t-shirt into a meaty tribute to Japan's rising sun flag.

DEMON THINGY

Gustav and his brother Alexander had been sat on the floor in the back of the white van for the last 30 minutes, monitoring the screen of Gustav's laptop. If it hadn't been for the coven's ritual room being two floors underground, they could probably have been back at the apartment and watching the footage remotely, but they had to be within proximity for the camera's signal to carry live images to them.

Viewed from the camera's hiding place in the corner of the Baker's Coven's chamber, Gustav and Alexander watched the hooded figures thrash and bray to their leader's incantations. Despite their hideous pronunciation, it seemed that the words had been successful.

"Zoom in," Alexander said.

Gustav did, and the screen closed on the coven's chubby leader, the wobbling cauldron, and a short, squat acolyte who appeared to be doing the Macarena.

"Be ready," Alexander said. "They might actually have managed something this time."

DEMON THINGY

Gustav's skin became hen-flesh. He dropped his sandwich and raised the crucifix pendant to his lips, praying for strength.

On the laptop, the black pot spewed thick smoke. The acolytes' chanting was interrupted by the congregation's coughs, hacks and wheezes.

Something shifted in the shadows of the smoke.

Gustav met his brother's eyes. "Should we..."

"Not yet. We need to be sure."

The shape revealed by the dispersing smoke gave the impression of a large football on legs.

"They've managed a successful conjuring," Gustav said. "I can't believe it."

Alexander remained silent, his full attention captured by the screen.

The smoke cleared and one of the acolytes – possibly that muscle-bound giant they called Dave – screamed shrilly.

On the laptop screen, the brothers beheld an abomination. Two thick appendages bulged and rippled, arm-like in appearance, but, rather than ending in fingers, each bore an extremity like a mishmash of a horse's hoof, a pig's trotter and either a human hand or foot. These strange arm-legs bore the weight of a spherical subnurnt-pink object, and a dark crevice split its form in two.

"What ... is ... that?" Gustav said.

The creature waddled off camera.

"Zoom out!" Alexander urged.

When Gustav did, the foul being reappeared.

"It..." Gustav said, before realising he was holding back laughter. "It looks like ... an arse!"

Alexander, generally solemn, especially when it came to their sacred mission, cracked a smile. "Yes brother," he agreed. "Straight from the bowels of hell!"

The pair creased up, and it was good. They had witnessed what they considered to be devilry and magical acts from the coven already, but this was several steps beyond. They laughed because of how unreal their lives had become. When they laughed, it was almost as if they were safe, and as if Alexander was not alive solely due to his brother's gift, and as if they hadn't just witnessed the conjuring of a true minion of Hell.

Gustav wiped his eyes with a meaty hand as his giggling fit faded. "Honestly. It's a good job that Lady Saffron is so inept, because otherwise she would be dangerous."

"She's not our problem, though," Alexander said, his narrow face and piercing dark eyes serious again. "It's this pair." He tapped the laptop screen's image of an odd-matched couple. "These two are the dangerous ones. Especially *her*."

9

The smell coming from the demon was atrocious, but Mrs Roberts supposed that she couldn't expect something fresh from Hell's nether regions to smell like the latest Jean Paul Gautier perfume. Its sideways mouth was lined with barbed teeth, and while there were no eyes to see, the thick black hairs emanating from its crack tested the air like antennae. It opened its mouth and the excremental stench tripled, causing the congregation to splutter and cry out.

Lady Saffron, who was still the only member of the group with her hood pulled down, looked repulsed. "It ... it's an abomination!" she cried, before adding, "And not in a good way!"

Mrs Roberts' heart clenched in her chest. It was a vile denizen from deepest Hades. It stank like a faecophile's breath. It was almost certainly dangerous.

DEMON THINGY

She would call it Sylvester.

The demon staggered further from the altar and the cauldron, grunting like a fat dog about to cum. Its whole being seemed to quiver like water ripples, then a low baritone rumbled from its botty-like gob. The sound ended with a high-pitched squeak, and something resembling a brown onion plopped onto the floor.

"The dirty bugger!" Clive shouted.

Lady Saffron took hold of the demon's hand-feet-hooves and dragged it towards her. "Someone gwab the knife out of my wobe!"

"No, Lady Saffron!" Mrs Roberts yelled. She wrestled the demon, whose teeth snapped like maracas, from Lady Saffron's wibbling grip. The creature let off another pungent guff.

"With the greatest respect, Lady Saffron," Mrs Roberts said, coughing and hugging Sylvester the demon to her chest. "While this isn't the being we had planned to summon from the void, it *is* a demon from Hell, and it could teach us more about the Dark One."

DEMON THINGY

"Stwangle it!" Lady Saffron trumpeted. "Wip it to pieces! It shat all over my coven fwoor!"

"Please, Lady Saffron..." Mrs Roberts tried again.

The other hooded coven members huddled around, but did not intervene.

Lady Saffron snatched at the beast once more, but Sylvester the demon's arm-leg tugged itself free and pressed one buttock against Mrs Roberts' breast, as if cowering from the lardy coven leader.

"I'm sewious! We didn't go to all this twouble just to summon fwatuwent postewior on wegs!"

"Lady ... *SAFFRON!!*" Mrs Roberts bellowed.

The coven leader froze, clutching her neck as if choking.

"Now," Mrs Roberts said, straightening her cowl. Sylvester found a comfortable spot to perch on her crooked arm. "I'm going to take it home and study it. Do some research. See what I can learn."

Lady Saffron's cheeks were red. Her eyes bulged. She gripped at her neck, as if trying to dislodge something.

Mrs Roberts asked, "Now, do you agree that this is a good plan of action?"

Lady Saffron nodded frantically, her face near-purple.

"Good," Mrs Roberts said.

Lady Saffron sucked in a giant gasp of air. Her impressive chest rose and fell, rose and fell, and despite her scowl, her cheeks were already losing some of their angry colour.

Mrs Roberts turned away from the coven leader. Her husband emerged from the shocked group of acolytes and joined her side. Sylvester farted softly, and for all the world it sounded like a cat's purr.

As they returned to the elevator, leaving the rest of the coven in silence, only Mrs Roberts

DEMON THINGY

saw the chubby straw doll her husband had slid back into his cloak sleeve.

DEMON THINGY

10

Something in the darkness smelled putrid, and it was probably the soggy thing draped over Clark's face. He felt it lift with each gasp of air.

Clark's limbs awoke gradually, as if the blood in his veins had turned to lumpy soup. The place where he lay was pitch black and reeking, but not entirely uncomfortable. He plucked up the courage to move one arm and unpeeled whatever was attached to his mouth and nose. It felt like some kind of vegetation.

There was a groan.

Clark gasped. The full stench of his surroundings hit his lungs: rancid piss, mould-ridden food, the eggy stodge of farts and the noxious fug of soiled garments.

"Clark?" a familiar voice echoed from somewhere nearby. "Where are we? Am I dead?"

DEMON THINGY

Everything fell into place at once. The foiled burglary. The poisoned hairpin. The chamberpot. The pair of old bastards. And now this wretched stinking darkness.

"No, you're not dead, Jackoby," Clark said. "You're just an idiot who's been beaten up, jizzed on, and chucked in a dumpster."

11

It had taken a while to drag themselves out of the skip, and Clark suspected that it would take a good few showers before they removed the stink from their hair and clothes. They'd traipsed back to their accommodation like a pair of incontinent, Buckfast-swigging tramps, reminding Clark of the days he'd lived on the streets with his late father. People had crossed the road just to avoid his dad and him, and the public done the same with Jackoby and Clark earlier that day.

Jackoby shuffled back into their bedroom of their measly budget accommodation wrapped in a grey towel. His hair was wet and his scrawny body still smelled of bins. Clark sat on the bed, rubbing his groggy head and picking at a suspicious-looking flake of crust on the bedsheet.

DEMON THINGY

"I think I should prob'ly go to the hopsicle," Jackoby said, looking like a morose weasel. "I'm all bust up."

Clark looked up. Jackoby's left eye had swelled shut. It looked like a ripened plum, ready to squeeze out its juices and shit its stone down his cheek.

"No no, Jackoby. Just grab a few paracetamols and you'll be fine."

"We haven't got any paracetamol."

"Well go out and nick some, then," Clark snapped.

Jackoby flopped down onto his side of the bed and sighed. "I can't *believe* that filthy fucker spunked on me."

"We don't know that for sure," Clark said, but he shivered at the thought.

"The filthy fucker." Jackoby sniffed. "We need some money."

Clark gave three sarcastic claps. "Observation always was your strong point."

DEMON THINGY

"How much of that weed do we have left to sell?"

"As much as you haven't smoked."

"Ah," Jackoby said. "Fuckballs." He coughed. "Ow. I'm hungry."

Clark shook his head. At least they had a roof at this point, which was more than his dad and him could have boasted for a few years. And at least, unlike his dad, Clark had resisted the lure of any harder habits than the dreamlike buzz of marijuana, whenever they had some to smoke. "We need a new scam, Jackoby," he said. "The cash we got from the old 'methy pineapples' gig has us covered to stay in this room for one week, starting tomorrow. Then that's it."

"Hmm. Only 12 more days, then," Jackoby said.

Clark let his head hang in despair. "We may have to go back to busking for a while, unless you want to try mugging someone again."

"I turned my flute into a pipe though. I don't know how I did it, but you've got to suck it to play a note instead of blow, now. It sounds terrible."

There was always suicide, if things got any worse for Clark. Just scrape together enough cash for a big old dose of heroin, and then off he'd float to fairyland to meet up with his dad again.

"Will it..." Jackoby began, letting his voice trail. "Will it *always* be like this?"

Clark didn't answer.

12

"Speak to me, I'm begging you," Mrs Roberts said, hating the pathetic whine in her tone. She rubbed her hands both nervously and because they ached.

It was early evening, after a long day. Mr Roberts was having a snooze in the lounge, and Sylvester the demon was curled up on his lap, apparently doing the same.

Meanwhile, kneeling in the dim haven of their alter room, Mrs Roberts was attempting to reconvene with the Old Horny Bastard. She had her best black candles burning, she was wearing her skimpiest black nightie, and she had a nice big tube of KY in preparation. Usually, the Great Dark Evil Chap would come to her unannounced and of his own volition, but since he had charged Mrs Roberts with the task of overthrowing Lady Saffron, she had decided to try and conjure the beast herself.

DEMON THINGY

She needed guidance. She needed reassurance. But most of all, she needed a nice long doodah slipped everywhere that it would fit.

Mrs Roberts had no idea how to progress in her mission of taking charge of the coven, and wondered if the incompetence of the other acolytes was worth controlling, anyway. Could she really snap them into shape, if she were to deal with Lady Saffron? How loyal were they to their current leader? Would such an ailing crew of crotchety devil worshippers be capable of ushering in the new Age of Darkness?

And, God bugger it, *when was her pink puffy engine going to receive another hot fuel injection?*

"I'm summoning you," she said through her clenched false teeth, which whistled over every 's' sound. "I need you to help me, please."

Nothing.

"What do you want, then?" she asked. "You want a sacrifice? You want a ritual? You want me to make you a nice naughty video?"

DEMON THINGY

Mrs Roberts tried to attune herself to the world's "other frequencies", listening with her cerebellum and watching the flickering candles with receptors beneath her skin. She closed her eyes, envisioning the beast's rippling flesh and great grasping hands pressed against her. The joy of it. The heretical horror of its touch.

"Please..." she yearned.

But the Grand Old Evil Chap never visited those who begged, unless his aim was to pick them apart like a Lego model. He only joined with those who were worthy of his throbbing organ, and the beastlike huff of his breath, and the thick, juicy squelch of his...

"Oh, bugger it all!" Mrs Roberts said, realising that getting all het up was not going to help her.

The only thing that would draw him to her again would be to do as she had been bidden.

Mrs Roberts may have been "mature", but when she raised herself to her feet there was barely a click of joints. It was her hands that were the problem, twisted and sore as they were with the buggery-bastard arthritis.

Time for another half-hour with The Stallion, she lamented.

She tugged on a cardigan, flicked on the light and began snuffing the candles with her fingers.

From outside the door came the now-familiar sound of Sylvester's gassy emissions.

Throughout the afternoon, as she had hunted through her arcane books and the darker corners of the internet, she had struggled to find a single reference to the existence of a demon such as Sylvester. There had been demons that had possessed people's posteriors, demons whose buttocks were used as weapons, demons who were so fat that they appeared buttock-like, but none quite like Sylvester. The strange creature they had summoned was a mystery, and as the day had worn on, Mrs Roberts had felt a connection growing between Sylvester and her, as if it was an important part of a puzzle she would one day solve.

DEMON THINGY

When she opened the door to their hall, her heart leapt in her chest.

Sylvester wasn't just grunting and breaking wind in its sleep.

Sylvester was trumping so frantically that it sounded as though it was *panicking*.

She rushed upstairs, realising that she could hear both Sylvester's rumbling trumps and her husband's frantic breathing and low muttered words.

Horace, if you've done anything stupid...

She flung open the bedroom door and saw Mr Horace Roberts doing something very bloody stupid indeed.

Sylvester was on the edge of the bed, struggling against Mr Roberts' grip which had the demon held firmly in place, its toothy maw facing her husband's crotch. Mr Roberts was naked from the waist down, his belly shuddering beneath his unbuttoned white shirt.

"Oh come on, please, just let me have a go. It'll be nice, honest."

DEMON THINGY

While it was clear that Sylvester could quite easily have used its jagged, horror-show teeth to chew through anything that her husband foolishly slipped into its face-bottom, the poor creature was tooting and honking in terror.

"Horace!" Mrs Roberts yelled.

Her husband's shocked face fell and he stopped moving. Sylvester scrambled from his grip and stumble-farted to the bedroom floor, trembling at Mrs Roberts' feet.

"This creature is not just another lodger you can molest at any moment you please!" she raged. "It's not just another burglar, or rent-boy, or vicar to penetrate with impunity!"

"But...Delia...I just..." Mr Roberts stammered.

"This beast has come to us from Hell itself, and no matter how strange it seems, and no matter how inviting you may find its appearance, it is to be treated as a revered house-guest. If I find you standing within 10 feet of Sylvester here, with or without that piddly little prick of yours on display, I'll suck the soul from your body."

DEMON THINGY

"Honestly, love, I..."

"Enough!" she thundered. She raised her hands, twirling her bent fingers into what looked like a complicated gang sign. *"Expungeous, Trevor MacDonald, flagellated VHS tracking, Delorian micropenis!"*

In the wake of those ancient words, her husband gave a groan, his jaw dropped, and with a gristly crunch he bent over at the waist. His cheeks fell into the rumpled bedding, his legs and arms tensed in unbearable spasm, and his entire body froze. He would remain that way, painfully locked in place, for several hours, or until Mrs Roberts decided to let him free.

Mrs Roberts crouched down to stroke the head of the cowering demon. There was no way that she could have called it "cute", but its pimpled buttocks and needle-like teeth appeared in no way threatening when it was pressed against her calves in fear. It was a creature she had been charged to protect, and as she ran her fingers across the upper part of its bum-skull, trying not to breathe its acrid smell, she could almost have believed that its panting farts were a repeated mantra of gratitude.

Thank you, it parped. *Thank you, thank you, thank you...*

"You're welcome," she said, trying to regulate her breath. "You must excuse my husband. He has certain distasteful desires that he finds difficult to resist. But you have no need to fear him now."

Sylvester stopped rubbing itself against her and "looked" up, the coarse hairs around its crack twitching curiously.

"I need to get myself some air, but I'll be back before you know it." She glanced up at her husband's folded form. "Now, I trust that you won't hurt him while I'm gone, Sylvester."

Mr Roberts groaned from the bed.

"Not badly, anyway."

13

From the bedroom, Edward shouted, "She just made him bend over, after he tried to shag the demon! This pair are more cuckoo than I thought!"

Alexander looked at his brother across the dining table and wiped borsch from his chin. "He's right, brother. They truly are demented."

Gustav managed to keep his face straight as he envisioned Mr Roberts trying to fornicate with the bum-demon. "When will we discuss our plan? How far will we let them go?"

"Soon, brother," Alexander said. "The time must be right, or we risk ruining everything."

Gustav felt anger. "How much worse can we allow them to get? They have already killed."

DEMON THINGY

Alexander took another calm spoonful of red soup. "Not directly, they haven't. Not to our knowledge, anyway."

"That is bull-*layno*, and you know it! It was murder, plain and simple!"

The Baker's Coven had come to the brothers' attention when they had witnessed Mrs Roberts' demonic witchery with their own eyes – and by Gustav's estimation, it had amounted to murder.

After leaving Pripyat with their mother when Gustav had been just five years old, they had travelled Europe, hunting for ways to use Gustav's incredible healing powers for the good of the world. Gustav could lay his hands on just about anything with a pulse, and within moments tell them what ailed them and either heal them entirely or at least reduce the symptoms of their pain. While their aim had always been to do good in God's name, Gustav's talents had also landed them an underground following, as well as the title, The Children of Chernobyl.

DEMON THINGY

It had only been as Gustav had grown older that he had revealed to his brother and mother that he had secretly been holding their own diseases at bay; tumours that had been growing within them since that fateful day back in Pripyat, after the Chernobyl disaster. Devastated by the revelation, Mummy Dudyk had insisted that he stop healing her immediately, claiming that there were far more worthy recipients of his gift. By now a grown man, Gustav respected her wish, but told her that he could not bear to watch her die. They had parted ways with their dying mother in a hospice in Frankfurt, deciding to seek out a quieter life by making their way to England, where they believed that news of Gustav's gift had not yet travelled.

Gustav had spent his 22nd birthday in a sealed shipping container at the Port of Felixstowe, and they had spent a year mourning their mother's death living quietly in a small village in the Midlands. They gained menial work, learned to drive, and liked to visit a variety of different houses of worship, trying to seek out the God who had granted Gustav with his gift. It had been during a trip to a Catholic Sunday service that they had first seen Mrs Roberts.

The middle-aged priest in the village of Boxford had been a brute of a man; broad, tall and bald. Mid-sermon, preaching from the pulpit, Father Sweeney became flustered and flushed. Gustav wondered what illness or ailment he suffered from, but resisted the urge to run to the front of the church and lay his hands on him, wishing keep their cover.

Father Sweeney leaned against the wooden pulpit, groaning in pain. Two choir members rushed from their seats to aid him, but Father Sweeney bellowed, "No stop!", his voice booming through the church. His expression was one of sheer horror as the two teenage choirgirls approached him, and he pulled himself upright in an unconvincing attempt to regain composure. Several congregation members cried out when Father Sweeney slipped down the half-dozen steps leading to the pulpit. When a couple of bystanders went to help again, he waved them away and refused to get to his feet, clutching at his groin.

DEMON THINGY

"I'm sorry!" Father Sweeney roared, as the persistent verger took one of his arms and the two teen choir girls grabbed the other. He fought and protested as they dragged him to his feet, and when they released him he was unable to hide a gigantic tented area at the front of his robes. The entire church gasped in shock when he pulled his vestments aside and revealed an abnormally engorged erection. Tears poured down his face and he screamed desperate apologies, but then seemed to give in. Gripping his balls with one hand and covering his eyes in obvious shame with the other, he machine-gunned strand after strand of semen into the face of one of the astonished choir girls, decorating her cheeks like strings of bejewelled garland.

Father Sweeney collapsed in post-orgasmic exhaustion, and the congregation erupted furiously.

Gustav had sensed that there were other powers at work, and scanned the church for something amiss. While all other eyes had been on the fallen, shamed priest, Gustav picked out the old woman with the white bun four seats to his right, and the waxen figure in her hands, complete with small penis and testicles. She was smirking as she slipped it back into her handbag, as was her large and sleazy-looking husband at her side.

The event had of course been scandalous, and the priest had been convicted of public indecency and sexual assault upon a minor. Father Sweeney had hanged himself in his cell, and his ashes had been used to summon the foul arse-demon whose birth Gustav and Alexander had witnessed earlier that day.

It was this event that had convinced the brothers that they had finally, unwittingly, discovered the holy mission that God had charged them with.

"It was murder, brother, and you know it," Gustav said. "And now they have successfully dragged something unholy from the underworld. So when, Alexander? When do we strike back?

Alexander swallowed another spoonful of soup. "When the time is right."

DEMON THINGY

Edward entered the dining room, staring at his phone. "I think, um, Gustav..."

Gustav glanced up, feeling irritable. "Yes, it's your turn again, isn't it."

Edward nodded, but didn't take his eyes from the phone. Gustav assumed that he was looking at the same picture of his baby daughter as he always did – the one where she lay asleep in her mother's arms, who herself lay exhausted and red-eyed in a hospital bed, just a few hours after the girl's birth.

"Come on then," Gustav said, rising from the table.

Edward looked up. "Can you...really cure me? For good, I mean?"

Gustav didn't nod, but simply said, "Give us the time we have asked of you. I do not lie."

Edward's face flooded with relief and, for just a moment, Gustav felt that everything might be alright, in the end.

DEMON THINGY

14

"Fuuuccking demon ssssod!" Seamus raged, firing a finger towards the pub roof and spraying his long grey beard with spittle. "Shhhowed you though, didn't I, you winged bastard? That'll ffccuukingg shows yoooou."

The staff at the Spam and Fag were used to Seamus, but tonight his behaviour was more unstable than usual. Seamus had spent the afternoon under psychic attack from the Nameless One, withstanding its attempts to drive him mad, crush his ego, or coax him into spilling his own guts over the kitchen floor. It hadn't mattered that Seamus had been down in his lounge, trying to study an ancient book about protection from demons, and the Nameless One had been upstairs and holed away in a portal of Seamus's own creation; the Nameless One had already delved into his brain, and that link gave it all the power the beast needed.

DEMON THINGY

Seamus ranted, "Any more of your puptooppee ... pitshit ... pituitary spells, an' I'd've had my brain on the other side o' my skull. But not ol' Seamusssss, eh? I did you once an' I'll will did you again."

Tonight was going to be a 12-pinter for Seamus; nothing aside from numbing oblivion was going to soothe the day's trauma.

"Another of those foaming bassssstardss, stout yeoman," Seamus called to the server, leaning against the bar and raising his empty tankard. It slipped from his fingers. He blinked, trying to follow its fall, but it bounced from the varnished wood and down to where it pranged his toe. The alcohol dulled the pain, but he still thought it would be best to sit down. He lowered his bony arse, missed the stall and collapsed to the sticky pub carpet.

"Do you think you've had enough yet, Seamus?" the bartender asked, in a tone suggesting that he understood the pointlessness of his question, but was going to ask it anyway.

DEMON THINGY

"Nnnnnnnnneever!" Seamus roared. "If a winged beast from Hell can't stop me, I'm damn sure that I can vanquisssssshhhh a bupple o' queers!"

"Yes, but you've had more than a *couple* of beers, haven't you?"

"Jssss fill me up, you rapsssssscallion," Seamus said, using the bar stall to tug himself to his feet. He lifted his mercifully unbroken tankard, spinning his other arm to keep upright, and waved the receptacle under the barkeep's nose. "Whhyy'd you keep movin' s'much?"

The bartender, standing stock still before the flailing geriatric, plucked the glass from his fingers and, with a laboured sigh, poured another pint. "Just one more. But if you break anything, or foul yourself again…"

"I've never fouled m'sssself," Seamus responded indignantly. "Piss issssss sterile – nothin' foul 'bout it."

"No fights, and no hassling women either."

DEMON THINGY

"How dare you, you imbertinent pounder?" Seamus yelled, snatching his drink and slopping a quarter of it down his front. "I'll haaave you know I'm a perfffffcect gentrymum."

"Well how disappointing," said a voice from behind him. It was high and scratchy, like a gramophone recording of a child. "Gentlemen are often so dull."

Seamus whirled around, squinting towards the pool table before lowering his head and meeting a woman's eyes. To Seamus, she looked like the attractive young blonde with the lively knockers from *Are You Being Served?* In truth, she probably looked more like the wrinkled old boiler with the knackered pussy from *Are You Being Served?*.

"Whhyyyyy, hello, my prrrrrretty," Seamus drooled, reaching out to shake her hand but instead prodding one of her bosoms.

Seamus's vision swirled and solidified for a few moments, revealing that the gorgeous maiden was a touch older than he had at first assumed, but no matter.

DEMON THINGY

The white-haired woman smiled two rows of beaming teeth, which contrasted alluringly with the haggard folds of her face. "You'd better get the other one too, or she'll only be jealous." She nodded down at her other gravity-bullied breast.

Pint eight was generally when Seamus's barely concealed sexual desperation kicked in. He was at an age when seducing a woman without payment was rarer than a cube-shaped turd, and, because of his condition, he had no way of achieving anything beyond some enthusiastic licking and slobbering, but this did nothing to suppress his desire for female company. Seamus raised his finger again and poked the woman's other nipple, like a doorbell. "My, my," Seamus burbled. "Aren't we a sssssstraight-talking husssssy?"

"I can be," she smiled, licking her thin, puckered lips. "I couldn't help but hear you talking earlier. Something about a 'winged beast'? Have you a new feathered pet?"

The questioned sobered Seamus momentarily. Had he been shouting? He had no idea, but he suddenly felt that it would be wise to stop blurting everything that came into his head. "Yessssss...a parrot. Called Beaky."

The woman leaned in towards Seamus. "If you tell me the truth," she mewled into his ear. "Maybe I'll show you what I can do when I don't have my teeth in."

She popped her dentures from her gob and smiled gummily, before slipping them seductively back into place.

Seamus gulped. "Wudju like a lil drinkie?"

"You really *are* a gentleman, aren't you?" she winked. "I'll have a gin and bitter lemon."

They drank. They chatted. Seamus struggled to keep upright before surreptitiously pissing himself. The woman, who referred to herself as Mrs Roberts, sipped her drink while Seamus spilled pints, and watched him order a bag of scampi fries before stuffing the reeking snacks beneath his robes. When she suggested that they went out to the alleyway beside the Spam and Fag, Seamus needed help walking straight. "Who are you again?" he asked her, as she pushed open the door.

Out in the fresh air, Seamus forgot about the woman holding his arm and began to stagger in the direction of the road. "Taaxxxxiii!" he bellowed, raising his arm in a Nazi-style salute to a passing car lit by the streetlights.

"Don't you want to come thish way firsht?" a voice asked. He turned and Mrs Roberts, a woman that Seamus had no recollection of having met, was waving a set of false teeth in the air beside her pinched, drawn-in cheek. She flapped her gums, arousing the intoxicated fragments of Seamus's brain, and then led him to the barely-lit alleyway.

Inside, lodged between an open skip and a brick wall, Mrs Roberts locked her lips sloppily around Seamus's. In his drunken daze, even if Seamus had been a complete man, he knew that he wouldn't have had a cow in an avalanche's chance of popping a stiff one; however, this didn't prevent him thrusting his tongue into the elderly woman's mouth and exploring her bare gums. The vinegary stink of her shampoo merged with the rotten cabbage aroma of the bins, dancing a tango with the dead-flower waft of her skin and the meaty gust of her breath. Seamus was in pissed-up sensory heaven.

Mrs Roberts pulled away. "Now," she told him, as he slid down the wall, eyes half-closed and bleary. "If you want to feel theesh gumsh wrapped around more than jusht your tongue, why don't you tell me more about your ... pet parrot?"

"Y'won't find mucccchh down there, sweetheart..." Seamus mumbled, and unzipped his trousers.

Mrs Roberts dipped to her knees, and reached into Seamus's zipper. The last thing he remembered before slipping into a drunken stupor right there in the alleyway was the look of utter confusion on Mrs Roberts' face.

15

After the disappointment of not getting a hot, hard, purple-headed winky rubbing against her gums and providing its own special Bongela to the sore bits, Mrs Roberts had changed tactics. She helped the drunkard, who called himself Seamus, locate a ride home after he goose-stepped up the centre of the road and failed to entice a single taxi driver.

A black cab pulled up before the pair, spraying puddle-muck up Seamus's trousers. To Mrs Roberts' surprise, a clean-cut man in a tuxedo was driving the thing, as if James Bond had commandeered a vehicle.

Seamus came around long enough to mutter something that sounded incomprehensible to her, but was obviously clear enough to the smartly-dressed driver, before throwing him a crumpled bank note and passing out with his beard mashed against the glass partition.

DEMON THINGY

Mrs Roberts climbed in beside Seamus and motioned for the hunky driver to do his job.

As the cab sped past pubs, clubs and greasy takeaways, Mrs Roberts wondered whether she was chasing this wildly drunken goose-stepper on a wildly drunken goose chase - but there was something about this bedraggled man that verily reeked of the occult. His pointed beard and battered fedora could have belonged to any old eccentric, but the scuffed brown robes he wore were oddly monk-like. And what she'd found – *or hadn't* – between his legs was bizarre to say the very least.

She inspected his snoring corpse as it dribbled brownly against the glass partition. A sliver of his lower back was exposed where his robes had ridden up, and she could make out the lower edges of an intricate tattoo. Ever the nosy old bag, Mrs Roberts leaned forwards for a closer inspection.

The depiction of a winged beast covered Seamus's wrinkled lower back. The wings were in four parts, like a dragonfly's, and in the translucent membrane were what appeared to be the screaming faces of numerous tortured, or at least dramatically constipated, souls. The glowing red body was insectoid, segmented in three parts, and its armoured abdomen tapered off into a barbed, twin-headed stinger. The head was fat and gelatinous, like a blobfish, and a huge drooping green moustache rested beneath the many eyes that riddled its hairless head like pock scars.

Mrs Roberts raised a hand to her mouth.

No one she knew had ever heard of Flick-Pigeon, The Eternal Tormentor of Zoophiles. It wasn't a name that cropped up at any of the Baker's Coven meetings, or at any of the Evil Coffee Mornings she frequented. She had only seen this image in one place before: in an ancient book of spells, conjurings and brownie recipes.

The image confirmed that this man had inside, first-hand knowledge of the deepest, darkest intimacies of the Netherworld. In short, he knew his shit.

When the taxi pulled up and the driver told her in an alluringly well-spoken accent that they had arrived, she pushed Seamus out of the vehicle and noted the address.

She pulled the door closed and eyed the driver, "Now, I need you to take me somewhere else."

The driver smoothed back his hair. "Where?"

Mrs Roberts smiled mischievously, "From behind, across these seats, and then back to my house for a night cap."

16

Seamus had always suffered from head-splitting, bowel-churning hangovers, and waking up the following morning on the kitchen floor in the same building as a multi-dimensional Hell-deity did nothing to soothe him.

He turned over, looked at the ceiling, and said, quite clearly, "Uuuuuuuugh ... mrgstrfquevob ..."

At the sound of these words, he realised that he was still completely clattered. If he felt as abysmal as this while still drunk, he was surely on course for a "morning after" of Lovecraftian intensity.

While Seamus knew a magickal trick or two (well, seven in total, to be precise), he had never discovered a spell or potion that settled a hangover more effectively that a few green grams of pipe-puffed skunk. He raised himself with a pained groan, his stomach rumbling like an outboard motor. Mid-rise, the horror of his situation peaked.

His head basically exploded.

With a farting squeak that sounded to Seamus like the trumpets of Armageddon, seven jets of liquid faeces erupted from his ears, nostrils, tear ducts and mouth, painting the kitchen brown as well as yesterday's clothes, which he still wore.

"Bugger," Seamus mumbled, through the depressingly familiar taste of his own excrement.

This was the first of Seamus's curses, which he had suffered ever since his first fateful encounter with the Nameless One: his digestive system now worked in reverse. He ate through his rectum, and every time he defecated it issued, not from his anus, but from the various holes in his head.

Two storeys above him, in another dimension, Seamus heard a noise through his diarrhoea-lubed ears: a peal of rasping laughter.

DEMON THINGY

"Oh, shut up," Seamus grumbled.

His knees crunched and complained as he dragged himself upright, using the kitchen counter for support.

Seamus remembered very little from the previous night, beyond sinking several barrels' worth of ale at the Spam and Fag. Aside from the vague memory of staggering through his front door in the early hours of the morning, there were just two other revelatory flashes: a cab drive home, and a stunningly gorgeous woman offering to mouth-massage his non-existent dick.

That was the second curse that the Nameless One had bestowed upon him, all those decades ago: the removal of his manhood.

The Nameless One tittered above him again, a sound that should not have carried so far but which seemed to echo through the corridors of his brain.

It was all too much to take, and he had a feeling that it wouldn't be long before the demon started its pituitary attacks again. Maybe a chilled

DEMON THINGY

smoke would sort his head, so Seamus hobbled to the phone.

17

Clark awoke to the buzzing of their shared phone on the bedside table. He sat up with a snuffle and slammed his face into Jackoby's sock-coated foot, which woke Jackoby with a start. At the sound of the ringtone, which rarely rang at all, fear creased Jackoby's face.

There were dozens of people who could have been ringing with obscene threats, or curious questions concerning their whereabouts and *then* obscene threats, but when Clark answered he realised that it was neither option.

"Hello?" a grizzled, hesitant voice said from the other end.

"Yes? What?" Clark demanded, furious to have been awoken from his peaceful sleep and returned to the hellish drudgery of penniless consciousness.

DEMON THINGY

"Are you the chap I met at the Spam and Fag the other night? The one who sold me that stinky cheese?"

"Cheese?" Clark asked, baffled. "What in fuck's name are you talking about? Who is this?"

"Seamus."

"WHO?!"

"Don't shout. My head feels like an old shoe."

Clark grumbled. "You speak to this old twat, would you, Jackoby?" He thrust the phone in Jackoby's direction, confused and annoyed. Maybe if he closed his eyes again he'd get to sleep. Perhaps he'd even dream about Susanna Reid dribbling custard down her cleavage again...

"Hello?" Jackoby squawked. "Oh, hello again, mate! Yes, the cheese, you liked it then? Mmm. Quality smoke, mate."

Clark's ears pricked up. The caller meant "cheese" of the green, smokeable kind, rather than the yellow, grateable sort. He must have been the crumbly old fellow who Jackoby had sold most of the rest of their weed to, the other night down the pub.

Jackoby continued, "No, we haven't got a..."

Clark nabbed the mobile from Jackoby's hand. "Yes, we haven't got any of the *cheese* left, but we've got some ... urm ... bubble-kush-custard-slap. It's, ah, even better."

"If it's green and puffable, I'll take it," said the voice down the line.

"Splendid. Where shall we meet you?"

"Do you deliver?" asked the voice, sounding weaker by the moment.

"Can do. Yes."

He handed the phone back to Jackoby. "Take his address down. Our luck has come in."

Jackoby covered the phone. "But we've run out, Clark."

"Don't you worry your pretty little head," Clark said. "I'll sort something out."

DEMON THINGY

18

Lady Saffron's eyes were wide with excitement as she stared over her takeaway Mocha Chocka Wocka Latte. She leaned against the alter in the dim coven room with Mrs Roberts standing beside her. A dozen or so acolytes, including the giant Dave and Beverly the blue-haired bint, had gathered in the pews. Mrs Roberts had called an emergency coven meeting, and was in the middle of describing the tattoo she had found on Seamus's back the night before, and why it was so important.

"And it was an accuwate image of Fuck-Pidgeon, you say?" Lady Saffron asked, half-hidden by a cup the size of a washing-up bowl, which brimmed with cream, foam, chocolate flakes, biscotti, coloured umbrellas and possibly somewhere coffee.

Mrs Roberts' lips quivered as she resisted the urge to roll her eyes. "Flick-Pigeon."

"Mmm, quite," Lady Saffron said. "Well, then we must awwange to meet up with this chap, mustn't we?"

"No," Mrs Roberts said firmly.

"Well, of course we will," Lady Saffron said, wiping a creamy moustache from her large face. "What an opportunity! Another occultist living nearby, ready to join forces with us!"

Mrs Roberts turned to the assembled coven members, who were dressed in their everyday clothes: cardigans, neat trousers, beige shirts, and flat caps. Mrs Merrel even had her duffel coat on, despite the warmth of the basement room. "We should put it to a vote, at least," she asserted. Before Lady Saffron could protest, Mrs Roberts said, "Flick-Pigeon, the Eternal Tormentor of Zoophiles, cannot be summoned by any means. It is strictly prohibited to leave Hell, and the only way that anyone would have seen such an image is in a book called 'Sex Magick – The Real Thing and None of That Fake Bollocks.'"

"Yes, I have a couple of copies at home," Lady Saffron said, slurping her coffee.

DEMON THINGY

"Lady Saffron," Mrs Roberts said. "There is but one copy. The original."

Lady Saffron opened her mouth to protest, but then closed it again.

Mrs Roberts continued, "The author of this book is almost entirely unheard of, but I understand that she was an ancient witch of immeasurable power. If what I have been told is true, she once managed to peek through Satan's gloryhole ... *and caught a glimpse inside.*"

Lady Saffron spluttered on her drink, splattering her forehead with foam. "You mean she ... actually saw into Hell?"

Mrs Roberts nodded. "And there she witnessed the entity known as Flick-Pigeon, The Eternal Tormentor of Zoophiles, doing his business."

"Having a poo?" snorted Clive, who was the only coven member still hidden beneath the hooded folds of his black robes.

Mrs Roberts scowled into the darkness where his face should have been. He may have been stupid, but he knew better than to say anything after one of Mrs Roberts' looks. His cowled shoulders slumped forwards and he looked back down into his lap.

"What I'm trying to say, Lady S, is that my drunken acquaintance is most certainly the real deal. And when he said quite clearly that he had captured a winged beast, I for one don't think he meant a fucking flamingo." Mrs Roberts grinned with malicious excitement. "And we all know that it is only Hell's upper hierarchy who are bestowed wings."

Lady Saffron froze, a cream-covered chocolate biscotti poised at her lips like the A-Team's Hannibal's cigar. "Mrs Woberts. This is incwedible news."

"Isn't it just?" Mrs Roberts said.

"So, now we are going to have to …" Lady Saffron began, before trailing off. Mrs Roberts was glaring at her, and Lady Saffron looked wary. "What… what do you pwopose we do, then?"

DEMON THINGY

Mrs Roberts kept her face straight, but Lady Saffron's acquiescence pleased her. "I propose that we go and get that demon thingy."

DEMON THINGY

19

Seamus had planned to head out and meet the loathsome pair of miscreants at the pub, but the thought of stepping outside feeling as bad as he did was unbearable. He had been pleased to learn that the two of them were content to pop over, so Seamus ignored a warning at the back of his skull and told them to bring him something green and stinky to his house, post-haste.

He almost puke-pooped again as he mopped the kitchen floor, but thoughts of high-grade herbs settled his stomach. He considered having a riffle through Father Nodsworth's Incantations and Stew Recipes in order to keep old Funny-Bollocks quiet upstairs, but he had no idea whether any of the mad monk's writings would have an effect on such a powerful being. Instead, he settled into the sofa and focused on feeling sorry for himself, and just hoped that the

DEMON THINGY

Nameless One would let his head be for a few hours.

When the drug dealers finally arrived, they looked just as wretched as Seamus felt: Jackoby, an IQ-starved lank-weasel, was dressed in army fatigues and smelled like acrid blue cheese. Clark was a short, sneering grub-merchant who dressed slightly neater and looked as though he would slice open his mother's stomach if she'd swallowed a quid.

At the door, Jackoby grinned a greeting. Clark nodded, avoiding Seamus's eyes, and picked an imaginary spot of fluff from his brown, flea-market suit.

"Come ye, come ye," Seamus said, and ushered them inside.

Jackoby's head almost brushed the doorframe as he entered. "You got any of that special tea we were talking about at the pub the other night?" he asked.

"Jackoby, where are your manners?" Clark hissed. His reptilian eyes darted from one side of Seamus's hall to the other, presumably searching for a valuable-looking volume to pinch amongst the ranks of piled books. He noticed Seamus noticing him. "But, out of interest...have you?"

Seamus smiled. "Perhaps I'll brew some after I've cleared my head with a much-needed pipe." He shuffled backwards and directed the motley duo into the cramped lounge. He kept his eyes fixed on Clark's hands, which the man had thrust into the pockets of his faded suit jacket.

"Averse to the idea of cleaning up, aren't we?" Clark said as he passed, wrinkling his nose.

Seamus ignored him and sat on his sofa with a groan. Jackoby rested his bony backside into one of Seamus's two armchairs as Clark frowned critically at his own seat, making a pantomime of brushing it before sitting down.

Seamus fished in his pocket and withdrew a £20 note. Clark's eyes gleamed at the sight of the money, and Jackoby even went as far as licking his lips, like a starving man eyeing a freshly baked pie. Seamus caught a glance shared between the pair and knew that something was wrong even before Clark held out the small baggy of green herbs.

"What's that?" Seamus asked, his hangover no longer abating. Instead, it had tightened his stomach like a vice.

Clark's face fell. "Thai sticks?" he said, the words more a question than a statement.

"I thought you said you had some bubblegum-kush-something-something?" Seamus snatched the baggy. "I may not know much about drugs, but aren't Thai sticks a little more...stick-like?"

"Not these ones," Jackoby squeaked. "They're, um, Jamaican ones."

"Jamaican Thai sticks?" Seamus said. He opened the baggy and inhaled. "They smell more Italian to me."

Clark's bold stature was deflating. "It's ... good shit?"

"Is it?" Seamus said, almost amused by the pair of chancers. "Good for getting high, or for flavouring a Bolognese?"

DEMON THINGY

Jackoby sighed. "I told you he wouldn't fall for it," he muttered.

Clark turned, a fierce warning on his face. Then perhaps he remembered just how much larger his companion was than him. "You never know," he said to Seamus, suddenly meek. "Oregano might work. Try it for a fiver?"

Seamus gazed at the shoddily-dressed pair. They both appeared malnourished and desperate. He groaned. "I'll make some tea."

DEMON THINGY

20

Clive waved goodbye to Lady Saffron and the Roberts, shouting a raucous, "See you in a bizzle!" as he left Pie-Eyed Bakery. His arms swung and his hooded cloak ruffled as he pranced up Walsall high street.

The passers-by that visibly stiffened when they saw him dressed like the Grim Reaper made him giggle; he always waved. A few weeks back, he had been standing at a bus stop behind an elderly man, who he had tapped on the shoulder three times. The wrinkled chap had turned around, gasped, and had a heart attack on the spot, his dentures exploding on the pavement as he'd fallen.

Cruel? Maybe.

Hilarious? Too fucking right.

Clive turned up a small street bereft of pedestrians, with just one little van parked outside a boarded-up restaurant. He span a circle to ensure that the area was deserted, stopped next to the van, rolled up one sleeve and rapped a knuckle against the side of the vehicle.

"Rudimentary paradigmatic erogenous salubrious shit nuggets," he said, through the side of his mouth.

The back door opened and a fat moustachioed man leaned out. "Ah Edward! Come in."

Clive tugged back his black hood and revealed his true identity: Edward, smiling a mouthful of pristine teeth. The sprightly alertness of his expression contrasted with the mindless idiocy of his Satan-worshipping alter ego, Clive. He climbed into the van, pulled off the black robes and folded them under his arm. Beneath the cloak, Edward wore a charcoal-grey suit, a white shirt, and a silver tie – a deliberate contrast to what the Baker's Coven probably assumed would be his dress sense.

Edward had agreed to "play" Clive after the Children of Chernobyl, as the brothers grandly called themselves, had put adverts up in the supermarkets and corner shops of Wolverhampton. Upon those decidedly lo-fi recruitment forms, they had written the following:

"Do you have something agonizing, ugly, or incurable? Have your doctors let you down? Have you run out of alternative therapies, and are looking for something real, AND FREE? Call us now for a consultation."

In the very week he had seen the brothers' notice, Edward's world had just collapsed around him. The doctor's words still buzzed in his ears, like placating yet professionally unemotional houseflies: *3 months.*

That's all he had, apparently.

3 months of meals, music, and movies.

3 months of masturbating and wishing he could make love to his wife to Maggie.

3 more months to spend with his beautiful new daughter Dorothy, aged barely 3 months herself.

That last part was the clincher; he'd been there at little Dorothy's birth. His wife was breastfeeding and had told Edward that it may be a while before she fancied indulging in some carnal fun again, but when she'd said that, Edward had told himself that he had plenty of time to wait for her.

Plenty of time.

Then, a few days later, a routine health check had found a tumour the size of a Big Mac in his guts, and Edward had felt his world implode. He had said nothing to his wife Maggie, and had secretly stopped going to the office to work. Instead, he had spent his usual work hours wandering the streets aimlessly and pondering how in the hell he was going to break the news to Maggie.

Strangely, the advert that the Children of Chernobyl had written and pasted up in Sainsbury's had been Edward's *very first* attempt at a cure, rather than a last resort as they'd suggested – almost as though it was meant to be. That was how Edward had become Clive: in exchange for infiltrating the coven and

DEMON THINGY

temporarily living alongside the Children of Chernobyl, Gustav had promised to heal him. Edward's wife Maggie had of course been horrified at the prospect of an "extended business trip", but she was surrounded by family to help. She would survive just fine, and when Edward returned, Gustav had promised that his tumour would be gone, and his family would be none the wiser.

In the van, Alexander and Gustav smiled and shook Edward's, nee Clive's, hand in turn.

"So, my good friend," Alexander said, his voice hushed. He looked drained, his eyes ringed grey and his skin pallid. The stress of their situation was no doubt taking its toll on his own condition. Edward already knew how it was to depend on Gustav for the good of his health, and while he had only been experiencing Gustav's powers for a few weeks, Alexander had needed them throughout his whole life.

Alexander added, "What an interesting turn of events. You weren't followed, were you?"

Edward raised a disbelieving eyebrow. "You should know better than that, Alexander. I've been pulling the wool over the coven's eyes for long enough now."

Gustav sat back down on the van floor and tapped at a computer keyboard connected to the van's surveillance system. "Shall I replay the footage?"

"No need," Edward said. "You were both watching Mrs Roberts speak? I'm waiting for her to text me, so I'll know when to meet with the others again."

Alexander joined his brother down on the floor, his face grave. "This goes far deeper than we thought, doesn't it?"

Edward rubbed a hand over his square jaw and leaned forward. "Mrs Roberts is more powerful than any of the other coven members. She's the ringleader, no matter what the other twits might think." He coughed into his fist and cleared his throat. Putting on Clive's loud imbecilic accent took its toll on him. "Now she thinks she's found a man who might have summoned his own demon. And this one is supposed to have wings."

"It's bollocks, Edward," Gustav said. "All this is ... is nonsense."

Alexander looked at his overweight brother, who closed his lips in response.

"But what if it isn't bollocks?" Alexander asked.

"I'd never have believed any of this, until a few weeks ago," Edward said. "I nearly ran at the first sight of that bloody arse demon!"

"We have already seen Mrs Roberts' black magic with our own eyes," Alexander said. "We have watched the coven condemn a man to torment, and then to death. And as Edward says, we have witnessed them summon a beast which has no right existing on God's green earth. So why must this new development be a lie?"

Gustav coughed. "Because in all the books we have read about the dark arts and conjuring evil spirits, we have only ever read that winged demons are ..."

"... Hell's royalty, yes," Alexander said. "My brother, we have passed the time for scepticism and denial. If there is even the slightest chance that what we have heard today is true, then we must go and investigate immediately." He glanced at Edward and back to Gustav. "The time for action is here."

Edward's pocket suddenly played a sample of Vincent Price stating, "The mark of Satan is upon them!" He took out his phone, and before he opened the text caught a glimpse of his daughter framed in the phone's background. He was doing this for her, and he'd soon be free to return to her. He opened the text message.

"Well?" Alexander asked. "What time are you to meet with her?"

Edward said, "Right now."

21

Clark spoke to Jackoby in a hushed voice. "Don't give me that look. You didn't have any better ideas, so what was I supposed to say? 'Sorry Seamus, we can't sort you out with any more gear, because we've smoked the lot, and we can't go back to Liverpool because my colleague invited our old supplier's daughter to a two-person bukkake party'?"

Jackoby screwed up his narrow face. "Parsley might have worked better."

"We didn't have any fucking parsley!" Clark hissed, as the kettle whistled in Seamus's kitchen. "Between us, our range of kitchen supplies included the oregano, one egg, a bottle of rancid milk, and two slices of brown bread. Oh, and a half-empty bottle of Fairy Liquid, which I've been using as shampoo for the past week. So, in the face of such a pathetic array, I think that the herbs were our best bloody bet!"

DEMON THINGY

Jackoby folded his arms and sent a gust of body odour Clark's way. "I'm starving."

Clark considered replying with an ego-crushing insult, but instead said, "There's always ... Plan B?"

Jackoby looked torn. "Aww, to Seamus? That's a bit harsh. He seems alright."

Clark countered, "Do you really want half an egg on toast for dinner?"

Jackoby shook his head. "Well *you're* going to the toilet this time, coz if anyone's getting hit on the head again, it's you."

"No one's getting smacked this time. And anyway, I hardly got off lightly last time, getting stabbed with that old bitch's hairpin!"

"Tea's here!" Seamus called, hobbling back into the lounge with a clinking tray of cups – one pink, one brown, and one yellow.

"Mmm, smells amazing," Clark said. "But I should probably go and clear out the old pipes before enjoying a brew."

DEMON THINGY

Seamus narrowed his age-hooded eyes and ran long fingers through his grey beard. "It's first on the right, up the stairs," he said, laying the tray down onto a table that was cluttered with more books, pencils, peanut shells, and an ornament shaped like a humanoid pig on a throne.

Clark nodded, trying so hard to look innocent as he stood up that he almost started to whistle. As he left the room, he heard Jackoby say, "So ... um ... read any good books lately?"

Clark followed the corridor round to the right and mounted the stairs. They creaked as he climbed and a dusty, cloying smell crept into his nose. Seamus's house wasn't large but it was certainly old. Drafts seemed to leak from the very walls. Up on the landing, Clark saw four unvarnished, unpainted doors, one of which led to the bathroom.

He tried to ignore a rare jab of guilt as he tried the closest door. The last time he remembered feeling such a jab was when they had dumped Old Eric into the reservoir, after he had threatened to go to the police about their "meth-filled pineapples" scam.

DEMON THINGY

The first door was locked.

Clark's heart sank. Seamus was eccentric but not stupid, so he probably had no intention of putting his valuable belongings at risk. Clark sighed. If only he had some way of escaping Jackoby, as well as this life of failed attempts to fuck people over, and meagre scams that rarely left him with enough cash for a Happy Meal.

He tried the other two doors; impassable.

Cunt-turnips.

The upstairs hallway was low and cramped, and the smell of age all-pervasive. There was something else too – some hint of incense or spiced herbs. Probably linked to Seamus's obsession with all that occult bollocks.

Clark ducked beneath a figurine about the size of a hand, which was suspended from the doorframe of the box-bathroom. It looked like a ragged scarecrow, and seemed to follow Clark with the small black marbles of its eyes.

While he was peeing into a toilet that was beige from grime, a noise from the landing outside cut him off mid-flow. It was the only sound he had heard since entering the bathroom: a creaking, but not of footsteps ascending ancient stairs.

Clark finished up and stepped back into the narrow hall.

The first door he had tried, beside the staircase, was now ajar.

"Seamus?" Clark asked, low enough so that anyone downstairs was unlikely to hear.

There was no reply, and only darkness between the crack in the doorway.

Could doors as old and worn as these just ... pop open? Didn't matter. What mattered was whether Clark could find something pawnable in the next few minutes, before Seamus grew suspicious.

In quiet haste, Clark used the torch from his mobile phone to illuminate the shadows through the door crack. He saw another set of steps, but shouldn't their direction have taken them through the house wall and *into the open air*, rather than towards a pitch-dark ascent into shadows?

He must have been mistaken.

He eased open the door. The dusty smell intensified but then gave way for something damper, but not like the damp of mould – more like the damp of the sea, or of a vast lake. For the first time Clark considered going back downstairs without seeking something to steal. Thoughts of a half-egg oregano omelette for dinner returned, though, and he stepped into the darkness.

The air was still as he ascended the time-worn wooden steps, but a denseness to the atmosphere reminded Clark of the times when Jackoby bought a copy of the Daily Sport to ogle: a humid warmth that suggested activities and truths that Clark would rather not acknowledge.

Clark crept further into the impossible gloom, sweeping his phone's torchlight ahead. He lit not roof rafters, but what appeared to be a moist cavern ceiling.

"Claaaaaaark…"

DEMON THINGY

A familiar voice meandered from the darkness ahead. Clark wanted to stop climbing but his feet refused.

He couldn't be hearing the voice of his late father.

"It's me, Clark. Promise you – promise you bad."

Promise you bad.

That's what his dad used to say, when Clark had been 10 and his mother had tossed both his dad and him out of the house. When they were taking refuge in an underpass or an alleyway, Clark would ask his father whether he had any money for food. "No son, I promise you – promise you bad," he'd say. But that hadn't stopped Clark from finding his father pale and motionless a few days later, propped up by a bin with a needle poking from his arm. Either his father had stolen whatever he'd put into that syringe, or he'd been lying to his only son and let him go hungry.

"Am I asleep?" Clark asked the lightless cavern, when he reached the top of the stairs. The stench of the sea combined with an offal-like scent. It made Clark imagine something split open and dead. "Did I drink Seamus's special tea already, and just forget?"

"No," his father's voice replied.

Clark turned his head towards the sound, and directed his torch the same way.

His father, unshaven, beanie cap pulled down over the back of his skull to frame his face, stood in the shadowed black with his spine pressed against a short pole. He was smiling, his uneven teeth glinting yellow, his eyes wide and welcoming. He opened his arms, and in the unnatural pale of Clark's torch Clark saw the old man's eyes moisten with joy.

"Son," his father said.

Clark wanted to step forward into those arms.

What kept him from the embrace was the multitude of dark red body parts scattered at his dad's feet.

Segments of arm and leg.

DEMON THINGY

Half a foot.

Toes and fingers pointing randomly.

A man's nipple, complete with a furry tuft of chest hair.

Three teeth.

A squashed eyeball.

"He wanted to hurt me," his father said, beckoning Clark with outstretched arms.

Clark found himself drawn, and when his shoes splashed stickily through a red pond he realised that he was pacing through dismembered remains towards a man who had been dead for over two decades.

"No!" someone bellowed.

"YESSSSSSSSS," the beast hissed through the darkness.

Suddenly Clark was no longer gazing at his long-dead father, but instead a grotesque, imp-like being, half his size with a curved horn sprouting from its forehead. It appeared to be balanced upon a metal pole. Level with Clark's waistline, crimson fire flared in its eye sockets. Its vulpine jaws snapped.

Clark squealed and dropped his phone. The only illumination became the thing's burning eyes, which cast orange needles across its gaping nostrils and the horn of its hairless head. Clark back-paced, and in the glow of its fiery gaze he saw it reach for him.

It surely meant to kill him.

"Ipso, facto, trumpety snatch-quack!" came a voice from behind Clark.

Clark heard a shriek, like a banshee, or like the sound Jackoby sometimes made during one of his private "Daily Sport" mornings.

Then everything went black.

Well, even blacker.

22

Mrs Roberts and the crew of crumbling Satan worshippers met at a traditional pub called The Priest's Tuxedo, and all 20 or so found themselves seats in the corner. They were dressed in their casual clothes for once – mainly a mixture of cardigans and flowery dresses. Well, all were casual, except for blue-haired Beverly, who had opted for a glamorous, sparkling green evening dress, big Dave, who wore thug boots, trouser suspenders and a checked Ben Sherman shirt that hugged his vast chest, and Clive, who was the only one in the room still wearing his usual robes.

Mrs Roberts bought them a round of gin and bitter lemons – it was all that most of them seemed to drink - and a rainbow-coloured alcopop for Clive.

"Enjoy your bridge game!" the barman laughed, until Mrs Roberts shot him a gaze that could have silenced a raging bull.

DEMON THINGY

Mrs Roberts sat down beside her husband, who had only suffered minor nips and nibbles to his legs and backside when she had left him at Sylvester's mercy.

A snuffled grunt came from Mrs Roberts' two-wheeled tartan shopping trolley. She lifted the top flap and patted Sylvester's head-bum. It issued a conspiratorial parp, which Mrs Roberts took to be good news. She withdrew a dead white mouse she had bought from a local pet shop and dropped it between Sylvester's buttock-cheeks. She zipped the lid closed to cover the sounds of the demon's satisfied crunching.

Lady Saffron was sat in the corner, looking both nervous and miffed. She wasn't used to having someone else act as leader. Mrs Roberts felt that she'd better bloody well get used to it.

"Now, acolytes," Mrs Roberts said.

"She just called them 'acolytes'!" the barman told the bleary drinkers propping up the bar.

Mrs Roberts ignored him. Best to stay as low-key as a gathering of ageing devil-worshippers could. "Clive, I told you to come incognito!"

Clive nodded his hood. "I did. You can't see my face!"

"That isn't weally what she meant, Cwive..."

"Thank you, Lady Saffron," Mrs Roberts said sharply. "Now, I apologise for calling you all to action at such short notice. You may end up simply sitting here for an hour or two before toddling home." She ran her eyes around the gathered subjects – soon to be *her* subjects – and raised a meaningful eyebrow. "But there is always the chance that we will go to war tonight. For now, though, I want you all to stay right here, and ready yourselves for my cue. Sylvester, Mr Roberts, and I will go and investigate the old drunkard's home, and see what there is to see. If we require assistance, you will hear from us. Is that understood?"

"Yes, but ..." Lady Saffron began.

"Good," Mrs Roberts said.

"I can come along, if you like, Mrs Roberts," Clive offered.

Mr Roberts' eyes lit up. "Oh, yes, maybe that would be ..."

"How kind, but no thank you, Clive," Mrs Roberts said. She rose, and signalled for Mr Roberts to do the same. He followed her as she dragged the shopping trolley from the pub. His head was low, just as it had been ever since his wife had left him paralysed with Sylvester.

The evening was dry and cool, the streets of Willenhall empty of both kids and the occasional travelling types who frequented its car parks. The dodgy-looking off-licences and Black Country pubs continued to issue a vague, unspoken aura of menace, but Mrs Roberts had nothing to fear when it came to her fellow humans.

"It's not far," Mrs Roberts told her trailing husband.

"Yes dear," Mr Roberts said.

He hadn't asked Mrs Roberts how she had met Seamus, and Mrs Roberts hadn't offered the information. They were both aware of the other's proclivities, and in general they kept them to themselves.

"What are we going to do when we get there?" Mr Roberts asked.

"I have it on good authority that we'll know once we arrive," she replied.

Throughout the day, while Mrs Roberts had been putting further research into the demon which Seamus had tattooed on his back, Sylvester had sat curled at her feet. At some point, Mrs Roberts had laid her head onto the desk in frustration at the lack of available information, and that had been when Sylvester's pong had hit her nose. She had opened her eyes and the weird little walking bum had been standing on its arm-legs a few inches away, as if watching her with its toothy arse-crack. She couldn't help but feel that, somehow, Sylvester had been trying to communicate, filling her mind with confidence in the path she was taking. Sylvester had popped out a turd the size of a Brazil nut onto the desk. Rather than becoming annoyed, Mrs Roberts had felt as though the creature was signalling something.

Once the pair reached Seamus's house, they waited behind an overgrown hedgerow for cover.

"Come on, round this way," Mrs Roberts said.

They circled the property using a narrow alleyway to lead them to the rear. Mrs Roberts stopped once they reached Seamus's back wall. A scrawled orange graffiti tag coated the brickwork, alongside an accusation targeting the apparent enormity of Charlotte Gilligan's vagina, whoever Charlotte Gilligan was.

"What now?" Mr Roberts whispered.

Mrs Roberts closed her eyes. She tuned in to the vibrations on the air, trying to sense the secrets that Seamus's non-descript house no doubt concealed.

Nothing.

Instead, Mrs Roberts unzipped her trolley, lifted Sylvester from his tartan confines and placed him on the ground. Sylvester leapt up onto its muscular arm-legs, wheezing and farting. It nuzzled at Mrs Roberts' handbag and pined like a begging dog.

Mrs Roberts crouched with a click of joints. "If you can help me, Sylvester, I'll get you a guinea pig to eat. That's several times larger than a mouse!"

Sylvester broke wind excitedly and ran around in a circle.

"You must be joking," Mr Roberts scoffed. "That thing might be a demon, but it's about as dumb as ... well ... an arse on legs."

Sylvester stopped running and looked up at Mr Roberts. When it clenched its head bum, it almost looked as though it was scowling. Then, in a clattering barrage of trumps, Sylvester issued a sticky, gloopy pile of shit so large that it was almost the size of the demon's bum-head.

"Oh, Christ!" Mr Roberts coughed, waving his hands frantically at the almighty stench.

Mrs Roberts' only movements were the rubbing of her arthritic hands. She was mesmerised.

Sylvester shuffled closer to the steaming brown tower, as if to sniff it. Then it leaned forwards.

Mr and Mrs Roberts both gasped when Sylvester plunged, head-bum first, into the poop, and promptly vanished.

23

Clark awoke with a snort and demanded, "Where'd that weed come from?"

Seamus's book-stuffed junkshop of a lounge drifted into view, and from the couch beside Clark, a red-eyed Jackoby coughed out a cloud of reeking herbal smoke.

"Oh yeah," Jackoby said. "You'll never believe this, but, um, I found a tiny little baggy in my …"

"You were holding out on me!" Clark snapped. "I sodding knew it. Give me that," he said, and snatched the single-skinned joint from Jackoby's hands. "*And* you've bummed the end," he tutted. He took a long drag.

"Would you like some tea?" Seamus asked, from the armchair across from Clark.

DEMON THINGY

At the sound of his voice, Clark was momentarily transported back to the impossible cave at the top of the stairs, and his father, and the thing that his father had become.

Clark's thin fingers trembled as he put the joint down into a round, clay ashtray. He felt as though he was standing on the brink of a precipice. He should take it easy, even with one of Jackoby's measly, prison-style spliffs. When Jackoby reached for it, Clark slapped his hand.

"What was that ... *thing* upstairs?" Clark asked.

"You were in its magical trance. You're lucky that I knew the right words to free you, or you'd be in pieces by now. That, or its slave." Seamus stroked his beard and kept his faded eyes on Clark. "You should never have seen it." He lifted his pipe – a foot-long, wooden contraption with several coils in its neck – and smoked. Pluming whorls of grey slipped from Seamus's cracked lips as he said, "It has no name."

Clark's natural response to fear was indignation. "Of course it has a name. Everything is called something. Is it so bloody useless that it doesn't deserve one?"

"The Nameless One has no name."

Clark was about to point out the contradiction within the claim, when Seamus added: "I should warn you that it can hear you, and it won't appreciate being called useless."

Clark shut his mouth. He glanced at Jackoby, who was staring at the spliff on the table. "Did you see it?" Clark asked.

"See what?"

"The ... bloody ... the thing upstairs."

"What? Oh, no. I heard it, though. Thought it was probably a dog or something." He sniffed. "You gonna pass that, yet?"

Clark shook his head and turned to Seamus. "So, out of interest, why do you have a dismembered corpse and a thing with no name up in a room that is actually a cave in what is, presumably, another dimension?"

"A corpse?" Jackoby gasped.

"*Yes!* He's got a chopped-up body and a creepy little monster upstairs!"

"The less you know, the better," Seamus said. "There's already one cadaver up there. I don't want any more."

"If it can hear me when I'm speaking," Clark said, "Then what else can it do? Smell me? See me? Hear my thoughts??"

"Perhaps," Seamus said. "Therefore, my advice is that you allow me to cast a minor enchantment and return you to blissful ignorance."

Jackoby jerked his head. "You aren't casting nothing on me. You could do anything in the meantime, and I've been through enough for one week, thanks. I didn't even see the bloody stupid thing, whatever it is."

"Sssshhhh," Clark urged. "It can hear you."

"No, it can't," Seamus corrected. "Jackoby's had no contact with The Nameless One, so it has no access to him."

DEMON THINGY

"Oh, great," Clark said. "So I'm 'marked', am I?" He sighed. "Look, I'm not a *'forget it all and just move on'* kind of guy. Give me the red pill, any day. And I mean the Matrix red pill, not the one eaten by those blokes who wank over frogs on the internet."

Seamus stared through a veil of smoke. "No. Either accept my offer, or get out."

Clark rose to his feet. "It's your fault that I saw the thing. So I think that the least you can do is fill me in on whatever it is I disturbed up there. Informed choice, and all that."

"I think I'm going to get out of here..." Jackoby muttered, getting to his feet as well.

Clark shoved the lanky bugger back into his seat. "You're in this just as much as I am."

Seamus's left eyebrow climbed so high that it seemed to float above his scalp. "What were you doing up there for so long, anyway?"

Clark hesitated. "Taking a leak, before that Nameless Thingy started calling me. Conjuring me."

DEMON THINGY

Seamus smoked and blew a grey ring as large as his head. His ear emitted a fart sound and an unholy stench filled the room. "Fine," Seamus said, "Sit down, shut up, and I'll tell you. Then, afterwards, I'm sure you'll *beg me* to let you forget."

DEMON THINGY

24

Gustav and Alexander sat on the floor of the van in silence, listening to two-dozen pensioners discussing cakes, whist, vaginal polyps, and how the *Daily Express* says that immigration causes cancer. Their faces were pale and taut with tension.

The brothers were parked a block down from the bar where the Baker's Coven sat. They had no video feed during this current stakeout, but they had given Edward, once again disguised as Clive, a wire to wear. They were both irritated at his half-hearted attempt at joining the Robertses on their journey to the old man's home.

Playing through an app on Alexander's phone, Edward's camp "Clive" voice rang out above the chatter: "Ooh, I think it's time to point Percy at the porcelain."

"Eh?" an unidentified devil worshipper asked.

"I'm having a piss," Edward clarified.

Alexander's phone transmitted the sounds of Edward making his way through the pub, presumably towards the bathroom. There was a clatter of a cubicle door closing and a white-noise crunch of Edward moving his mic to speak directly into it.

"I'm going to follow them," Edward said.

In the van, the brothers looked at each other.

"I don't know why, but I feel ... strange," Gustav told his brother. "Like this is where things have been leading for a while. Mrs Roberts has become more confident with her authority, and I'm worried. This is the first time we've known them to do something as direct as this."

"I know what you mean," Alexander admitted. His eye sockets were smudged rings.

Gustav worried that it was not only the day's stresses that had caused his brother to appear so deathly. "Do you feel okay? Should I give you some healing?"

"There's no time today, brother. You should also prepare for the worst - I doubt they coven would have called an emergency meeting without a good reason."

"This is madness," Gustav said.

"I know," Alexander said. "Will you be able to protect us, if you have to?"

Gustav tried to sound optimistic. "I'm sure it won't come to that."

Alexander shook his head and cleared his throat. "We are here to vanquish the darkness, and to spread the word of truth."

"Amen," Gustav replied. He put a hand around the back of Alexander's neck and pulled his brother towards him, so their foreheads were touching.

"We are charged to rid the world of evil," Alexander said.

"Amen!" Gustav replied.

Then, in unison: "We are the Children of Chernobyl."

Gustav released his frail brother and kissed the crucifix around his neck. "Now let's go."

25

"...and in two months' time, I'll have my knob back."

Seamus signalled that his tale had come to an end by taking a bourbon biscuit from the table, reaching down the seat of his trousers and slipping the chocolatey snack up into his back passage.

"Oh, Jesus Christ, Seamus," Clark complained.

"Look, you know the truth now, so there's no need for me to pretend to be normal anymore."

Seamus was surprised to find that it felt good to have gotten everything off his chest. He'd spent 50-odd years getting pissed, casting mostly useless spells and never telling anyone about his burning desire to correct his anatomy and slaughter that damned Nameless bastard - but now he'd finally shared his secrets.

Yes, he had a crater for a penis.

Yes, he ate through his arse and crapped through his head.

But all that was going to change, because he had successfully cast what could be the most impressive summoning spell in the history of humanity, and trapped the little fucker in a secret chamber of his own creation. *That* would show those plebs at the National Master Mage and Spiffing Sorceress's Guild.

"So ... let me get this straight," said Jackoby, who had perked up during Seamus's story, listening like an attentive kid. "You can drink through your mouth, but you have to eat through your bum?"

Before Seamus could reconfirm this fact to Jackoby for the fifth or sixth time, Clark said, "Is that really your most burning question? The message you took from this story of interdimensional beings, decades-old vengeance and supernatural powers is that 'Seamus poops weird'?"

"Yes, Jackoby," Seamus said, exasperated. "So if The Nameless One can do that to me with one click of its fingers, imagine what it could do with five clicks? Ten? Imagine over the course of your lifetime the torments it could inflict upon you!"

Clark's eyes twinkled in a way that Seamus didn't care for. His mouth was a wild rictus. "Yeah. But imagine what *good* you could make it do, if you kept it trapped." Clark licked his lips, popped the joint between them, relit it and folded his arms as he puffed. "Well, screw it. You know what? I'm in."

Seamus drew back. "'In'?"

"Yup. I want money," Clark said.

"Are you mental?" Jackoby asked. "It could kill us."

"I want birds with comically massive wanger-bangers."

"Clark, I don't know what you..." Seamus began.

"I want power. Magical abilities." Clark took the spliff from his gob and blew smoke in Jackoby's face. "An endless supply of the best weed in the world, *only better*."

Jackoby's eyes seemed to clear. "Hmm."

"Come on, what else have we got going for us?" Clark asked Jackoby. "An eternity of bad scams and miserable failures. Getting beaten up, living on the brink of starvation, and shifting from shithole to shithole, stuck in each other's' pockets."

"Well, I quite like living with you, Clark..."

"*Well I fucking don't!*" Clark snapped. "We're grown men! We shouldn't have to be this way!"

Seamus felt his face falling, his heart sinking, and all sorts of other metaphors that described fear and discontent.

"I want to visit other countries," Clark continued. "Other planets. I want to read minds and fly, and breathe underwater. I want to turn into a panther." Clark puffed the joint again and screwed up his face before passing it to Jackoby. "So if you want to keep smoking 95%-tobacco doobies for the rest of your days, Jackoby, then that's fine. But I'd rather *become a Goddamned God.*"

Seamus smirked at the thought of this strange pair being granted omnipotence; it was preposterous. But while he had no idea of the extent of the Nameless One's abilities, Clark was right about its vast potential. Seamus had been so consumed by the desire to regrow his todger that the idea of anything beyond that had barely occurred to him - but now he understood what Clark's face telegraphed: there was much more at play here. Clark and Jackoby might not have had much altruism at heart, but Seamus was suddenly struck by a thought so potent that it almost felt like a premonition.

What if someone else got their hands on the Nameless One?

Seamus's skin chilled. He had always known that there was a chance that the demon could escape his magickal snare and condemn him to either a horrendous death or infinite suffering, but he had always supposed that, afterwards, the beast would simply slink off to its own realm, just as it had following Seamus's last encounter with it.

"So, what do I do?" Clark asked Seamus, having apparently completed the list of demands he would reel off to the demon, if given half the chance. "I mean, to help. I'm offering you our services."

Seamus was about to guffaw and sneer at the offer, when something inside his head, just beside his left earlobe but beneath his skull, began to throb. At first he thought that it was going to be another cranial bowel movement, or perhaps another pituitary attack, but this sensation was different. It was tighter, less physical, more ... ethereal.

It was the Nameless One.

And it was a warning.

26

The Robertses waited in the alleyway by their demonic pet's basketball-sized pile of shite. Mr Roberts tapped at his phone and Mrs Roberts rubbed her hands, willing her arthritis to give it a bloody rest. The pair were hardly great conversationalists at the best of times, but following the previous day's events they had barely exchanged a word.

A ginger-haired chap wearing a One Direction t-shirt and sandals passed them by with a Jack Russel on a lead. The dog took a sniff of Sylvester's turds and gave a yelp. It scampered ahead, tugging the lead to urge its owner to move faster down the alley.

Just a few moments after the man had rounded the alley corner and escaped from view, there was a bubbly pop and the huge brown deposit seemed to snuffle to itself. One smeared arm-leg appeared, followed by a second, one on either side of the crap. With a strain and a gurgle, Sylvester's botty-body appeared from the impossible depths of the muck.

"Sylvester!" Mrs Roberts cried, relieved at the beast's safe return. She realised that she was rather fond of the repulsive little thing.

Sylvester, smudged from finger-toe to arse-cranium in its own faeces, hopped about her feet frantically.

"Is it trying to tell us something?" Mr Roberts asked.

Mrs Roberts scowled. "I believe it most certainly is."

Sylvester tooted in an almost nervous manner, grabbing fistfuls of grass from the edges of the wall and flinging them towards the excrement. Then it leapt up into the air, nodding its *tete-derriere* in the direction of the wall hiding them from Seamus's tall house.

"What's it mean?" Mr Roberts said.

Mrs Roberts sighed. "Horace Roberts. What did I ever do to deserve a dullard such as you?"

DEMON THINGY

She began to undress, peeling off her cardigan and the several layers beneath it.

"Delia!" Mr Roberts gasped. "What are you doing?"

In a few moments, she was standing in her birthday suit, which she had to admit was in need of a good iron. "Okay, Sylvester," she said, and crouched before her pet. "Let's do this."

Sylvester stood to attention, his arm-legs taut and muscular, their feet-hands planted firmly on the floor. His whole form began to quiver and a long, low baritone gas emission vibrated through him to emerge from his widening rectum-mouth. The crack down the centre of his face spread apart, and the multitude of needlepoint teeth retracted into its flesh. His throat-anus – encrusted with shit, rodent residue and only Satan knew what else – slackened. The noise increased in volume. Green gas erupted from the opening, its tendrils wrapping around Mrs Roberts' face, cooling and numbing wherever they touched. There, amidst Sylvester's reeking breath, Mrs Roberts felt understanding rush into her like an intravenous injection of pure, terrifying knowledge.

Unable to see anything but the green smoke, Mrs Roberts reached forwards and felt what could only be the gloop of Sylvester's defecation. Her fingertips plunged inside, and as she slipped further forwards, her wrists and her elbows and her upper arms becoming submerged in the supernatural sludge, she said to her husband, who she could no longer see, "Call the others...we need each and every one of them here."

Then, when she felt her face immersed, everything became starlight.

27

"Can you feel that?" Gustav asked his brother, as they quick-paced along the roadside. "Like a ... like something pushing against your eyes and ears?"

"Like pressure before a storm?" Alexander asked. "No. But you have always been more sensitive than me."

This was true, but this afternoon Gustav felt more than just sensitive – he felt *electrified*.

"No, brother," Gustav said. "Not like a storm. More like when a plane flies overhead, but as if the plane isn't heading through the skies, but ... towards me."

The Baker's Coven's meeting place pub was a block ahead, and Edward was waiting for them on the corner. He had already stripped off his robe and hood and was back in his usual business suit. "Lady Saffron gave us the address, so let's go."

Edward's paces were far longer and quicker than the brothers, who struggled to keep up - particularly Alexander, who was wheezing and holding his sides.

"I think that this is more important than the coven, guys," Edward said, over his shoulder. "I think that it's bigger than them killing Father Sweeney, or summoning that arse-thing or..."

"I know, Edward," Gustav said, impressed at how much his new friend had come to care about the operation. "I feel it too."

Edward stopped. "Can you protect us?" he asked. "I mean, *really* protect us?"

"There it is," Alexander pointed, enabling Gustav to dodge giving an answer. "That's the address."

28

Mrs Roberts soared through a blazing, blinding realm, as something unseen told her the secrets of the universe.

She'd never been the "druggy" type, but this was just how she imagined it would be like after munching on a couple of cocaine pills.

Except bigger.

And brighter.

And much weirder.

It wasn't just the glorious light she saw, either. Through her brain there marched ecstatic visions of unparalleled oddness and scale.

In awe – true, paralysing, mind-bursting awe - Mrs Roberts watched a gelatinous blob the size of a planet sculpt a galaxy, with the sounds of squelching mud.

DEMON THINGY

She saw a vast being of indeterminate shape (though she thought she caught a flash of writhing tentacles and stumpy green wings) scowl up at the Earth, from a dead city lying impossible leagues beneath the ocean.

She witnessed two opposing deities, one the colour of blood and the other the tone of a storm-cluttered sky, bickering, in strident howls that would have crushed her very mind if had she been anywhere other than here ... wherever here was.

As a spectator, she saw the universe expand from "nothing" to become what humans called "everything", before retracting backwards and consuming itself whole.

Beyond all these and many other sights and wonders, Mrs Roberts recognised that the only reason she was seeing them was due to Sylvester, the preposterous, arse-faced demon who that twerp Lady Saffron would have killed if Mrs Roberts hadn't stopped her. Somehow, Sylvester was revealing things that she needed to know in order to triumph against Lady Saffron, and against this other demon that Seamus had

DEMON THINGY

conjured – and perhaps even against the Grand Dark Horny Sod, if it came down to it.

Now *there* was a thought: making the Devil Himself grovel at her feet and then servicing her naughty bits, whenever and wherever she commanded.

More and more visions came to her: of gods, of demons, of unknown depths and unfathomable heights, of secret crevices and venomous dimensions, of the meaninglessness of good and evil, and of the contradictory insignificance and yet eternal importance of the human race, and then...

POP.

She saw two fiery eyes, a skinny grey body, and a weak-looking pair of wings. With a hideous, creeping realisation, Mrs Roberts had an idea that nothing she had ever witnessed – even this psychic tsunami of insanity-inducing visions – could have existed, if not for this frail-looking beast that now stood before her.

And Seamus had somehow ensnared and enslaved him.

DEMON THINGY

With this recognition, all became dark.

Mrs Roberts was surrounded by something wet, warm and slimy, and she couldn't breathe. She crawled forwards, through the glop clogging her nose and mouth, and at last emerged into a cavernous, barely-lit aperture. The roof bore disturbing stalactites that dripped slime to the rocky ground where she now lay, and Mrs Roberts sensed that wherever she was, it wasn't quite Walsall anymore.

Something tittered, childlike, behind her.

Mrs Roberts knew that whatever she was about to see was going to change her, perhaps forever. Her stomach felt like unset jelly but she told herself to harden, to find strength in her years of having practised the dark arts and studied their potential, and to remember that she had succeeded in summoning *and fucking* the devil Himself, so she was certainly a match for this decrepit little gremlin, no matter how impressive its CV was.

She was ready to put all this knowledge into practice, and to face a new opponent.

DEMON THINGY

It was time to do battle.

DEMON THINGY

29

Clark could see that Seamus wanted rid of them, but he was having none of it.

"You both need to leave," Seamus said, his bones popping like bubble-wrap as he rose from his chair. "Something is ... happening."

"Didn't you hear what I said?" Clark said. "You've made us a part of this, whether you like it or not."

"I'm not 100% sure ..." Jackoby started.

"*Well, how about you just fuck off then?*" Clark hissed.

Jackoby jumped, spitting out the spliff.

Clark'd had enough of his partner-in-slime. If Jackoby was too much of a pissy-knickered woofter to come along for the ride, then it would be his loss, not Clark's.

DEMON THINGY

Seamus was already half-way to the lounge door, ushering Clark and Jackoby from the room. "Come on. Shoo. Out. Things are about to get ugly."

Clark followed him and stopped, crossing his arms stubbornly and making no attempt to head for the door.

Seamus looked at him and sighed. "It's your funeral."

"What's wrong?" Jackoby asked.

"The Nameless One. I believe it's calling me." Seamus's eyes narrowed. "But it feels different. Like there's some other kind of threat."

"Maybe it's given up," Jackoby said, picking up the sorry remains of his joint and popping it behind his ear. "Maybe it's going to give you your knob back, and you won't have to wait those 66 days, after all."

"Oh, so you were listening, then?" Clark said, as Seamus led them upstairs.

At the top, Clark began to feel queasy. The door he had opened before was ajar, but the

DEMON THINGY

darkness behind it was different, now. Redder. And there were noises.

Seamus mumbled as they walked. At first, Clark assumed that it was an incantation, but when he leaned in towards Seamus's shoulder, the old wizard was humming an off-key rendition of the Countdown theme.

"Look," Seamus said, at the door. "Neither of you idiots should be following me up here, but I have a feeling that you're going to regardless."

"You just want to make that thing your personal slave," Clark said. "Well, I want some of the action, too."

Seamus raised his milky eyes. "Just stay quiet, the pair of you."

"Do you have some kind of ... weapon?" Jackoby asked.

Seamus pulled open the door and revealed shadows tinted by a dull but fiery glow. "Oh sure. I've got a magical demon-slaying bazooka in my back pocket."

A pause.

DEMON THINGY

"Really?" Jackoby asked.

"No. I have my words. That is all."

Seamus began to climb stairs that should not have been there. When Clark passed through the door, he saw that the fragile-looking wooden steps themselves were aglow, and he became lightheaded as they climbed. It was fair to say that Clark was an impulsive fellow – why else would he find himself regretting most of his decisions? – But when it came to matters of bravery and sheer balls he wanted to be known as a chap who rarely backed down. He glanced at Jackoby behind him, whose bean-pole-thin features were touched by the ominous illumination of the stairs. Clark had been hoping that Jackoby would appear nervous, giving Clark the chance to abandon the plan while blaming his *friend's* fear rather than his own. Sadly, Jackoby looked as dense as ever. He even grinned.

The noises from above were clearer now. They made Clark imagine fireworks zooming high above a farmyard orgy.

DEMON THINGY

When he neared the top of the 20-or-so stairs, Seamus held a hand back at them. Clark slowed his pace. The weird groans and honking detonations from above were as confusing as they were unnerving, and their volume had grown as they'd climbed. The weird crimson incandescence coming from the stairs now glowed and flashed with the light from whatever was happening in the cave-room.

When Seamus reached the summit and turned left into the chamber, Clark saw an expression hijack the man's face that would haunt his dreams to come. While the old man's body became a statue, his eyes seemed to retract into his skull, as if denying what they had already seen. His lips curled back from his teeth and his nostrils seemed to swallow his nose.

Finally, Clark's curiosity overwhelmed his terror, and he bounded up the final few steps.

The hums, crackles and booms were louder at the top, but not overwhelming. The cavernous interior was lit by disturbing, strobe-like glares that switched colour and intensity with each second. They emanated from the centre of the cave where two figures, surrounded by electric-blue sparks and a buzzing storm of yellows and greens, appeared locked in war – *coital war*.

The room's demonic captive, which Clark had already briefly seen, was not *balanced* on the pole, as he had at first thought – it was anally impaled by it. The haggard grey form, as thin as a starving child and yet somehow all the more terrifying for it, had been confronted by a nude crone on all fours. Her head, which bore an oddly familiar white bun, was positioned before the creature's knee-high groin, her skull slurping back and forth. The pair grunted and whinnied in frenzy. The face of that demon thingy was the most disturbing sight of all: twin streams of red light were firing from its eyes like ghastly headlamps, and its long jaw gaped, lop-sided, as if lost somewhere between ecstasy and terror.

The thought of anything that could overpower a creature like that made Clark want to surrender there and then.

Seamus drew back and bellowed, *"Expellio, flange-kopf, disabled parking zone!"*

DEMON THINGY

The crouching hag turned, a half-sneer, half-smile, stretched across her face, and a grey, pencil-thin protrusion entering her mouth.

Clark and Jackoby gasped. "You?" they said together.

The woman, who Clark last remembered pushing a hairpin into his throat before presumably allowing her husband to spunk over their unconscious bodies, drew her head back. The grey pencil-thing – the demon's dong – plopped from her wrinkled gob. The sparking and whistling colours died, as if rudely interrupted, so that the only light in the room now came from the demon's glowing red eyes.

Keeping one sturdy arm planted to the floor, the old woman lifted her other hand to her lips and slipped a pair of dentures in. "Nice to get my lips around something stiff for a change."

Seamus expelled a shocked breath, firing his own dentures to the stony ground. "You..."

The demon was still, its mouth wide and its eyes burning bright, angry – *yet somehow fearful.*

DEMON THINGY

"You don't know what you're doing!" Seamus yelled gummily, reaching down for his teeth.

The woman glowered. "I know more than you ever will, you cockless old fool."

"How did you find me? How do you know about the Nameless One?" Seamus demanded, and then frowned. "Do I know you?"

"Is your memory as absent as your winky?" the woman asked.

"Move out of the way," Jackoby said from behind Clark. "What's going on? I want to see."

"Just run!" Clark told him.

"No one will be running anywhere," said the old woman. Still on all fours, she looked up at the demon's slack face. "Bring him to me."

Jackoby barged past Clark.

"What are you doing?" Clark asked.

Jackoby's feet were locked side-by-side but he was moving at a pace. Clark grabbed his friend's arm. At the touch of his hand a pink spark leapt from Jackoby's shabby jacket. Clark yelped and released him.

"Ah, Stooge number 3," the woman gloated.

"What's going on?" Jackoby asked, still drifting forwards. "Did ... did you spike my tea, Seamus?"

Seamus scowled. "I'm afraid not."

When Jackoby was within reaching distance, the old woman rose to her feet. Jackoby whimpered, in a distressed way that only a man whose limbs have been controlled by a naked old witch can whimper.

"Give her a left, Jackoby!" Clark suggested.

"A left what?" Jackoby asked.

"You're making a terrible mistake, woman," Seamus said. "That creature wields more power in its left testicle than you do in your entire body!"

Lit by the red glare of the demon's powerful eyes, the old woman smirked. "Tell me: what is more powerful – the nuclear submarine, or the crew that commands it?"

"An elegant metaphor," Seamus admitted. "But very few military weapons would force their crew to saw off their own tits and eat them, if given half the chance."

The woman's face flickered, but the only emotion it showed was triumph.

30

From the outside, the old man's house appeared as normal as any suburban West Midlands home, except more banged-up and a great deal older. An end-of-terrace in need of some TLC, its three storeys stood innocently against the afternoon sun, as if secreting nothing more significant than a family chobbling their cobs and a couple of bostin' cups of tea.

Gustav knew it was the right place. His nausea seemed to have travelled all the way to his fingers and toes, as though his very nails wanted to vomit. He could feel what he thought of as "waves of wrongness" throbbing from the building. They reminded him of the choked air of his home city of Pripyat, shortly after the disaster. Was this where his life had been leading this whole time?

Was this why God had granted him such unique abilities? To thwart evil, now and forever?

And was the ability to heal the only gift he had been given – or was there more?

"What do we do?" Edward asked, looking as unnerved as Gustav felt. His tie had somehow travelled to "4 o'clock" on his neck, and his usually neat hair had become eccentric.

"Circle the building," Alexander advised. He was trying to sound authoritative, but he looked terrible. His shadowed eyes flitted distractedly, as if he'd spotted the Grim Reaper across the room but was avoiding eye contact. "See if anything seems amiss."

"Everything feels amiss," Gustav muttered, his skin crawling and his stomach feeling several tons too heavy.

Gustav focused, reaching out with his mind to seek the source of his discomfort. He could feel ... something ... lurking at the edges of his understanding. He had never used his brain in such a way, but he supposed that he had always known that his powers went beyond the telekinetic ability to heal. He had only hesitated to explore them because he felt that he needed permission from God to do so.

As Alexander led them down the alleyway that bordered the building, Gustav pushed his awareness further, urging it onwards, somehow knowing that Mrs Roberts was close but sensing that something stood between them, preventing him from reaching her.

He knew one thing for sure: this new development wasn't a "load of bollocks", as he'd once suggested. Whatever the old man had trapped in his house was as real as real could be.

Near the alleyway's first turn, an unpleasant smell accosted them. Gustav held his nose, the stink and the sickness that the house emitted teaming up on him.

Edward, the tallest of the trio, stood on tiptoes and peeked over the wall. He shrugged. "Can't see anything unusual. It's just an overgrown garden with a few funny-looking figurines."

"Gods? Demons?" Alexander asked. "Maybe a portal to another realm?"

Edward squinted. "I think they're just gnomes."

There was a sound from around the corner – a low rumble – and Gustav, Alexander and Edward gagged. A pair of eyes appeared from around the turning, just a few metres from Alexander, and then vanished.

"Hello?" Alexander called.

"Bugger off!" a man cried.

Alexander reached the corner.

His face met a large, meaty fist.

Alexander careened backwards.

"Shit!" Gustav said, rushing to his brother's side to hold him up. He turned and saw Mr Roberts blowing on his knuckles.

"Come on then, busters!" Mr Roberts said, putting up his wrinkly dukes. "We'll take you all on!"

"We?" Gustav asked.

DEMON THINGY

Sylvester, the demonic arse on arm-legs, stalked out from behind Mr Roberts, squatting its limbs as if to warm them up.

"Who are you?" Mr Roberts demanded.

"They're the Children of Chernobyl," Edward said, joining Gustav's side.

"Clive?" Mr Roberts asked, a frown creasing his face.

"I suppose the game's up, then," Edward said, and ploughed a fist into Mr Robert's cheek.

The old man collapsed in a geriatric heap, his head landing backwards with a squelch into what appeared to be a giant pile of faeces.

Sylvester farted at such a low pitch that it sounded like a growl, and then leapt. The demon may have been a knee-high pair of buttocks on limbs, but when Sylvester hit Edward's stomach, Edward almost crumpled with the impact. His long arms span like lop-sided swing-balls and he stumbled, but managed to remain standing. Sylvester was not yet done with him, and launched itself once more. Edward grunted at the second blow but stood firm, crouching and clapping a hand onto either side of the demon's face-arse. Like foreplay shot from the world's most disturbing porn scene, Sylvester's cheeks spread open and revealed two sets of uneven, gnashing jaws.

"Do something, brother!" Alexander told Gustav, weakly.

Gustav dashed forwards a few steps and aimed a punt at one of Sylvester's cheeks.

His boot connected with one of Edward's hands, instead.

"Oh, I'm so sorry!"

As Edward flinched his left hand away, Sylvester span its mouth around and chewed into Edward's right sleeve. Edward squealed, for a moment truly sounding like his camp alter-ego Clive, and shook his arm with the beast still attached. The creature guffed aggressively, its rectal mouth rimmed with Edward's blood and its own excrement.

DEMON THINGY

"Get it off me!" Edward wailed. "Oh God, get it off!"

Green gas spouted from Sylvester's maw, but the demon held firm.

Mr Roberts lay dazed on the ground. Alexander seemed to have been rendered useless by the old man's sucker-punch and stood shivering against the wall. That left Gustav to deal with the reeking monster alone, so he raised his boot and brought it down hard onto Sylvester. A squeak of green gas burst from the snaggle-toothed hole and Edward's arm was released, bleeding heavily. Edward grit his teeth but didn't cry out. Sylvester's limbs wobbled like the legs of a bodybuilder heaving a weight bar overhead. The demon took a step backwards and then collapsed.

"We should get out of here!" Edward panicked.

"No," Gustav said.

"I need a hospital," Edward said, clutching his bloodied wrist.

"I said no! There's too much at stake!"

"How do you know?!" Edward protested. "You said yourself that it's all probably just bollocks, so..."

Gustav felt something dark cross his face. Edward closed his lips. Gustav's psychic nerve endings were twitching wildly, facts and disparate truths slotting inevitably into place. He could sense things more acutely than ever before. He could do more than just heal – much more.

He knew things.

"Help me keep this fucker still," Gustav said.

Although Edward was clearly in pain and losing blood, he reacted as if taking an order from a superior officer. Whimpering, Edward shuffled forwards and gave Sylvester a firm kick to one of its arm-legs. The beast buckled and fell to one knee-elbow. Edward stepped one foot onto each of the creature's wrist-ankles, keeping it in place.

Gustav crouched down, holding his breath as panicked green fart-gas huffed from Sylvester's vile teeth. Gustav followed a weird instinct: he pressed his hands against Sylvester's pimpled cheeks, pulling them apart as wide as he could. More green gas drifted out, but with its bum-cheeks spread, the demon's trumps were no longer sounds of baritone flatulence, but panicked panting noises.

"Come on, you little bastard," Gustav said, as they held the beast firm. "Show me what you've got."

The gas slowly dispersed. Gustav gazed into the creature's fanged and splattered arse-gob, and there, deep inside its anal gullet, he saw Mrs Roberts, nude, and something else. Something grey, malignant, and immeasurably powerful that made his skin tighten and his consciousness wish to recoil. He saw an old man, the house's owner, bleeding on the floor, and two other figures stood in opposition to the crone and the demon.

He did not know if he was seeing a premonition or just a vision of another place, but he realised in that moment that this grey, nameless demon was something that Gustav and his brother would have to destroy. If not, the world would face consequences that Gustav hardly dared consider.

DEMON THINGY

Then, Edward's torso fell off.

31

From the darkness at Clark's side, Seamus released an ear-stabbing shriek. In everyday circumstances, the idea of a wizened old duffer making such a noise would have seemed unusual, but in the face of the Nameless One's stare it was the only rational response. That, plus the fact that Seamus's arm had been twisted almost 360 degrees and raised into the air.

Clark's survival instincts from having lived on the streets and conning and cheating his way through life were useless here, in this gloomy, dripping cavern.

The old woman stared dispassionately at Jackoby, who still stood before her, arms limp and hanging like a marionette. Rubbing her hands together, she asked, almost gleefully, "Would you like us to pull your leg from its socket, or to chew it off at the knee?"

Jackoby, a lanky silhouette facing away from Clark, made a wet noise of terror.

The old woman said, "I'm giving you the choice. You should thank me."

Clark watched, tempted to try and flee but gripped by a weird aversion; perhaps the demon's magic or the old woman's influence.

"Fine," the woman said, in response to Jackoby's silence. She turned to the Nameless One. "Awaken."

The glow from the demon's headlamp-eyes dimmed. The cave-room lost light and the creature seemed to gain a modicum of awareness. It snapped its jaws and flexed its snout.

Jackoby slobbered again; a sound that Clark had heard him make before in times of danger.

"Let them go!" Seamus yelled, his hand still raised with its fingers spread-eagled. "They're nobodies. They're nothing."

It was no time for indignation, despite Clark's natural tendencies. He was way out of his depth here, and for once he was big enough and ugly enough to admit it.

"*Moorhen, raddicio, dulux pastry...*" the old hag said, rising to her feet and squaring up to Jackoby with her forehead no higher than his nipples. "*Ballsack, farmhouse cheddar accumulation ...*"

"Don't!" Seamus squalled. "Please, just –"

Distracted, the woman turned to Seamus and spat, "*Extracurricular fuck-chimney!*"

There was a dull boom, like the combination of an explosion on TV and a gong being bonged.

Seamus squealed.

Clark winced at the chewed-gristle noise of Seamus's arm being wrenched even higher. It popped from its socket. There was a jolt and, with a lumpy splurt and a 4-way squitter of blood, the limb, ragged sleeve and all, tore away from Seamus's body. Seamus screamed again and collapsed, holding a hand over the place where his arm had been just a second before.

DEMON THINGY

"Jesus fucking Christ!" Clark yelled, turning to the exit.

Something tapped Clark's shoulder. He turned.

Seamus's severed arm floated before him, its fingers curled into a fist.

"None of you have a clue of the powers I now wield!" the old biddy roared.

Seamus's levitating hand, its arm-stump still dripping, raised its middle finger. Clark was about to run when its forefinger arose in a victory "V" and rammed both digits up into Clark's nostrils. The pain was horrifying; Clark felt like a hooked fish. His eyes gushed as the hand rotated him back to face the woman and the demon. Clark kept his hands at his sides, afraid of his nose ripping away from his face if he fought back. When the fingers began to drag him across the room, his vision was too water-blurred and the pain too intense to resist. Blind, he let himself be led, his feet splashing through what must have been a rapidly growing pool of Seamus's blood.

DEMON THINGY

Through his tears, Clark saw the grey creature ready to attack but apparently awaiting its cue from the lady, like a wretched guard dog.

The nude old woman smiled without a trace of kindness. "Don't worry, little things. You'll be better off this way in the end."

The hand stopped pulling Clark when he reached Jackoby's side.

The old woman stood before them, with the Nameless One poised to pounce just a step behind her. Its red eyes flashed, and Seamus whimpered in the gloom.

The old woman turned back. "Now, demon," she said. "As your god ... I command you: destroy them."

DEMON THINGY

32

"Where in the *hell* have you been hiding that sword?" Mr Roberts asked, sitting up and staring at something behind Gustav. His wispy hair was clogged brown from the shit-pile he'd fallen into.

"Had it down the back of my shirt," said a squeaky voice.

Gustav had raised his hands and remained frozen ever since Edward's upper body had thud-splattered to the floor. "He had a child!" Gustav bellowed.

Edward's legs had continued to stand on Sylvester's limbs for a second after the attack, then they had fallen, one to the left and one to the right. Edward's torso lay on its back, the space where his thighs and crotch had once been now a bleeding, bone-splintered mess. Edward blinked. A bubble of gore popped in one nostril.

"Stop ... them," he said, his lips spilling runnels of red. "You're ... the ... children of Cher ... Cher ..."

"*We* are the children of Chernobyl," Gustav hissed, gripped by grief but knowing that to give in to it would mean death.

"Try to ... reverse it ..." Edward gasped. He coughed up a chunk of something gristly, one eye rolled upwards and the other rolled down, and he died with a dramatic splutter.

"Reverse what?" Gustav asked, blinking back tears.

Mr Roberts dragged himself up with a groan, rubbing turd-lumps from his hair like thick, brown dandruff. "That was a good right hook he had," Mr Roberts said. He looked up at whoever was standing behind Clark. "Shame you had to cut through his arse, though, David. That was Clive, didn't you know? Even dead, I bet he would *still* have made a great shag."

Gustav turned slowly around, keeping his hands raised. He closed his eyes, terrified of what he might be about to see.

DEMON THINGY

He opened them.

His brother Alexander was alive. A crumbly-looking woman with a blue perm and a rumpled scowl had him by the scruff of the neck. Even in his frail condition, he still looked as though he could have shaken her hands off – but there was a hulking beast of a man wearing typical skinhead gear stood between Gustav and Alexander, holding a dripping samurai sword in a fist the size of a ham hock. There was also a handful of the other ageing acolytes dressed in their everyday clothes, staring around the alleyway in a decidedly unthreatening manner.

"Now," Mr Roberts said to Gustav. "Stand up. Dave here will make sure you don't do anything inadvisable."

The vast man nodded and rubbed his beard. "Yeah," he said, his voice was high, like a child's.

Gustav arose from Sylvester's body, picturing what he had just seen between Sylvester's spread cheeks. "Do you know … what's happening in that house?"

DEMON THINGY

Mr Roberts scoffed. "Wouldn't you like to know? Now …"

"Your wife is playing with forces more powerful and malevolent than you can imagine."

Mr Roberts laughed. "Listen, pal. We're *devil worshippers*. That means we don't give a demon's dick about what you consider 'evil'."

"What did you see, brother?" Alexander asked.

"Shut it," Mr Roberts said. The soprano-voiced beast-man he had called Dave raised the sword.

"No!" Gustav cried. "Please. We'll do as you say. I just don't think you realise what will happen if she manages to win – or even if she loses."

"Win?" Mr Roberts asked. "Against the demon thingy?"

Gustav smiled. "Maybe."

Mr Roberts smiled back, but his was infinitely more unpleasant. "Cut him, Dave."

DEMON THINGY

Gustav lifted his hands higher. "Okay! Okay! I'll tell you!"

Dave turned to Mr Roberts. Mr Roberts nodded. "Go on, then."

"The old man is hurt."

Mr Roberts' grin widened. "Good."

"But he's got company." Gustav then tried to be smart without appearing disobedient, adding, "And they're fighting back."

Mr Roberts' grin evaporated. He narrowed his eyes, apparently deciding that Gustav was telling the truth - or that it was at least worth bothering to find out for sure. "Dave. Give Beverly your sword and come with me. *Now.* Sylvester!"

The little arse demon stood up unsteadily. It shook its botty-head like a wet dog.

"Make sure they don't follow us, or get away."

The creature nodded, and Mr Roberts and Dave hurried out of the alleyway.

DEMON THINGY

Beverly, the woman who'd been holding Alexander by the throat, wobbled the sword in Gustav's direction. "Now don't you be causing any trouble, or I'll unzip your ballsack with this thing."

"Is it true, brother?" Alexander asked.

The remaining acolytes murmured but showed no aggression.

Gustav lowered his head. "Yes. But I think she has control of the situation. I think she's going to win."

"Could Edward have been right?"

"What do you mean?"

Beverly shook the sword again. "You two had better shut your pie-holes."

"Can't you try to ... reverse it?" Alexander asked.

Something popped in Gustav's brain, like a lightbulb, only brighter and more energy-efficient.

Sylvester fart-growled at his feet.

DEMON THINGY

"No. There's nothing," Gustav said, but he thought that he understood.

He concentrated.

He concentrated on the space between Sylvester's cheeks, and the portal that led to Mrs Roberts and the demon.

He concentrated, he prayed, and focused the only idea he had.

DEMON THINGY

33

Through his pain and terror, Clark watched as the Nameless One's long jaws tightened in apparent delight. Its bat-like wings spread as wide as its arms and it rose, the pole slipping from its backside with a squeak of flesh against metal. Its eyes brightened once again, but this time, rather than being aware and hateful, they appeared hypnotised. It stepped forwards.

"Bleeze," Clark said, attempting to beg with Seamus's fingers still stuck in his nose. "Bleeze doan 'ur dim..."

The waist-high creature stared up at Jackoby. It was shorter than the old woman, but Clark's head swam as he stared into the glowing horror of its eyes.

"Sit," the woman said.

The demon sat immediately.

DEMON THINGY

Rubbing her gnarled hands, the crone flashed a yellow smile. "Stand."

The demon arose.

"Open your mouth."

Clark almost felt sorry for the creature, terrified of it as he was. The Nameless One was a beast that appeared accustomed to its own agency, and the idea of this naked, dangle-boobed biddy ordering it about seemed unjust. The creature's long, wolfish gob fell open.

"Push your face into his crotch," the woman said.

Clark was nauseated. The frustration and disappointment he often felt for his friend were considerable, but as pathetic as Jackoby was, he didn't deserve this.

"Oh God," Jackoby mumbled, still frozen in place. "Oh please God, no …"

"Do you have the little worm's little worm between your teeth?" the woman asked, sweetly.

DEMON THINGY

The creature nodded, the end of its jaws pressed against Jackoby's flies.

"Good," she said. "Now...uurrrggjyiuyithhgtgegttsggghhhs!"

At first, Clark took the sound to be another of the woman's spells, despite the sound being even more nonsensical than her previous incantations. However, the demon thingy's mouth remained open.

The old woman started to shake, and Clark saw that her hands had curled into themselves, like a frail bird's feet gripping a branch. She was looking in horror at her fingers, her hands raised in disbelief, her lips open and panting.

There was a sound not unlike the creak of an old gate, and the end knuckle of one of her forefingers jerked sideways. She screamed. One pinkie inflated with a pop, and the wrist of her other arm seemed to collapse in on itself.

Clark did not understand what he was seeing, but her digits appeared to have become a wretched parody of a terrible case of arthritis.

DEMON THINGY

"Oh, make it stop!" the woman screeched.

One by one, the old woman's fingers bent and swelled, until she was moaning one long, pathetic whine of pain. Both her hands resembled complicated knots of rope as she fell backwards, still staring in shock at her ballooning knuckles.

What the hell was going on?

Seamus's severed arm fell, its fingers slipping from Clark's nose. It hit the floor and did not move. Though Clark's nostrils ran with blood, he did not think that he'd suffered any permanent damage.

"Can I ..." Jackoby started. "Can I step back now?"

He was looking down at the Nameless One, which was still waiting, pre-chomp.

"Do it," a voice wheezed from the darkness. "Do it quickly."

"Seamus?" Clark asked, his face throbbing.

"Yes," the old man breathed.

DEMON THINGY

Jackoby stepped backwards, and the front of his trousers emerged from the creature's mouth.

The Nameless One's red eyes crawled up to Clark, but its body did not move.

"You can't ... get away!" the old woman shrieked, from the ground. Her twisted hands shuddered at her sides, and then gave a snap. She screamed, the noise wracked with agony.

"Quiet, woman," Seamus muttered. "Did you do this?" he asked, perhaps to the Nameless One, but there was not reply.

Clark turned. Seamus had sat up but looked delirious, his eyes rolling in his head. The place where his arm used to be was a bloodied, trickling hole. Clark could see part of his collarbone protruding. He would be dead soon, Clark was sure of it.

There was still strength in him yet, though. "Now listen, you two."

DEMON THINGY

Clark took another look at the Nameless One, which was still motionless. He and Jackoby stepped closer to hear what Seamus had to say.

"There is only one thing that we can do." He clutched his shoulder and his hand turned red. "The way I see it, we have but one choice: fight, or perish."

Clark thought that Seamus had no option aside from the latter, but then again it almost appeared that the bleeding had slowed. Some kind of wizardry, maybe.

"Jackoby," Seamus said.

"Yeah?" Jackoby replied, his voice lunatic with panic.

"Calm down. Focus. There is a book in my bedroom that you need to fetch. Look behind the headboard, and you'll find a wall carving of Dame Edna Everage."

"*What?*"

"Don't ask, just listen! Press her nose and you will find a secret compartment. Ignore everything else that you find there, but take the book entitled 'Sex Magick'."

Jackoby hurried off down the stairs, his departure accompanied by the old woman's petrified groans of pain. Clark bristled with jealousy at the fact that Seamus had chosen Clark's buffoonish partner for the job instead of him, but said nothing.

"Come closer," Seamus said. "I need to instruct you. I need to prepare you ... for the worst."

There was a distant pounding.

"Seamus! Clark!" came Jackoby's voice. "I think someone's trying to bust down your front door!"

"*Then hurry!*" Seamus yelled. His eyes glazed but his voice held firm. "This is your only chance, Clark. I'm going to perform a one-off spell. You need to remember what I've told you – every detail, if you can. If you do, you won't just be saving yourselves, but many other people, too. Perhaps everyone."

DEMON THINGY

"What ... what do you want me to do?"

"You have to keep the Nameless One trapped for the remaining 64 days."

"Clark, help!" Jackoby bellowed,

"Do you have the book?!" Seamus called.

"Yes, but they're inside and there's no lock on the landing door!"

Seamus hurried on. "You need to stop these people from finding the Nameless One, and you need to keep the demon helpless and imprisoned until those 66 days and 6 hours are up, and then it will become our slave."

Clark glanced back at the demon. Its eyes glowed dully. "Won't he stay like this, now?"

Seamus shook his head gravely. "This is temporary. The Nameless One cannot be stopped forever – merely numbed for a short while. And whatever power this woman thinks she has over him, she's wrong. Without the book, she has no way of keeping him under her control."

DEMON THINGY

"Ha! That's what you bloody think!" the woman cackled suddenly. "Demon! Kill them all!"

But her words seemed to have lost their effect over it.

"How can we get out of here?" Clark asked.

"I can see to that," Seamus said. "But only if you trust me."

Clark saw no other option. "Just do what you need to do."

"Pleeeease!" Jackoby shrilled.

"Go and hold the door," Seamus told Clark. "I'll see to things up here. Then, when I call you, come back up and do exactly as I say."

Clark rushed from the cave-room and down the stairs. Jackoby was pressed against the door that led to Seamus's house, which was juddering with repeated blows from the other side.

"Jesus, God!" Clark yelled.

"God has no place here!" called a voice from behind the door.

There was a slam and the door shook as if it was going to explode.

"Move over," Clark said, and when Jackoby shuffled sideways Clark pushed himself against the wood.

"You can't hold us off forever!" the voice came again, and Clark felt a shiver of familiarity. Was that Mr Roberts? "We'll be in there soon, so you might as well let us in now. Harder, Dave!"

"It's ... it's him," Jackoby said. "It's the one who ..."

"Just hold the fucking door!" Clark said.

There was another crash, and the blow felt more powerful than a single person could have mustered. *"WE'RE COMING FOR YOU!"* squealed what sounded like a child's voice.

"Clark! Jackoby!" yelled Seamus. "Get up here at once!"

"If we leave the door, they'll get in!" Clark shouted.

"Get up here, *NOW!*"

DEMON THINGY

Clark locked eyes with Jackoby.

Jackoby said, "You go first."

Clark, stricken with terror and certain that he was about to be either eaten, dismembered, or buggered to death, pulled away from the door. He was about to run back up the stairs when he saw a look pass over Jackoby's face.

Jackoby wrenched open the door. Mr Roberts, a face from a nightmare, stood beside a looming monster of a man. Jackoby flung his fist through the door. Mr Roberts' eyes screwed shut and his nose exploded gorily.

"Have that, you dirty prick!" Jackoby said, and slammed the door again. "*Nobody* cums on Jackoby S. Flindenheim!"

Clark pelted up the stairs with Jackoby's footsteps in pursuit.

Something in the cavern-like room whirred like a propeller.

Seamus stood a few feet from the top of the stairs. His shoulder seemed to have all but stopped bleeding. Impossible, but an everyday occurrence compared to the shape awaiting them in the spot where the Nameless One had been trapped, just moments before.

There was a circular portal, floating mid-air. A liquid darkness that swirled like a whirlpool.

The demon stood before it, still passive.

Clark could no longer see the woman.

"Do you have the book?" Seamus asked.

"I've got it," Jackoby panted, holding up an old-looking tome.

There was a commotion on the stairs behind them. Yelling. Thumps and curses. Mr Roberts and his Igor-like assistant would be up there in moments.

Seamus said, "Grab the Nameless One, remember everything I've said, use the book to protect yourselves and follow its directions *to the letter*. Now go!"

Clark was almost as afraid of the vortex as he was of the demon, of the old woman, of Mr

Roberts, of... well, of everything within reaching distance, except for Jackoby.

Jackoby didn't look at Clark for confirmation this time: he raced towards the Nameless One, scooped it under his arm as if he was lifting a kid, and jumped into the portal. Clark saw a flash of a strange, tear-like symbol on the demon's back, and then the pair vanished with a hiss.

"*GO, CLARK!*" Seamus urged.

Heavy footsteps raced up the stairs.

Clark's face was in agony, his brain in turmoil.

Everything was a blur.

Clark sprinted eight steps and sprang; face first, into the cold, black unknown.

DEMON THINGY

Author Biographies

MATTHEW CASH

Matthew Cash, or Matty-Bob Cash as he is known to most, was born and raised in in Suffolk; which is the setting for his debut novel Pinprick. He is compiler and editor of Death By Chocolate, a chocoholic horror Anthology, Sparks, the 12Days: STOCKING FILLERS Anthology, and it's subsequent yearly annuals and has numerous releases on Kindle and several collections in paperback.

In 2016 he started his own label Burdizzo Books, with the intention of compiling and releasing charity anthologies a few times a year. He is currently working on numerous projects, his second novel FUR will hopefully be launched 2018.

He has always written stories since he first learnt to write and most, although not all tend to slip into the many layered murky depths of the Horror genre.

His influences ranged from when he first started reading to Present day are, to name but a small select few; Roald Dahl, James Herbert, Clive Barker, Stephen King, Stephen Laws, and more recently he enjoys Adam Nevill, F.R Tallis, Michael Bray, Gary Fry, William Meikle and Iain Rob Wright (who featured Matty-Bob in his famous A-Z of Horror title M is For Matty-Bob, plus Matthew wrote his own version of events which was included as a bonus).

He is a father of two, a husband of one and a zoo keeper of numerous fur babies.

You can find him here:

www.facebook.com/pinprickbymatthewcash

https://www.amazon.co.uk/-/e/B010MQTWKK

DEMON THINGY

Other Releases By Matthew Cash

Novels
Virgin And The Hunter
Pinprick

Novellas
Ankle Biters
KrackerJack
Illness
Hell And Sebastian
Waiting For Godfrey
Deadbeard
The Cat Came Back
Krackerjack 2

Short Stories
Why Can't I Be You?
Slugs And Snails And Puppydog Tails
OldTimers
Hunt The C*nt

Anthologies Compiled and Edited By Matthew Cash

Death By Chocolate
12 Days: STOCKING FILLERS
12 Days: 2016 Anthology
12 Days: 2017 [with Em Dehaney]
The Reverend Burdizzo's Hymn Book (with Em Dehaney)
Sparks [with Em Dehaney]

Anthologies Featuring Matthew Cash
Rejected For Content 3: Vicious Vengeance
JEApers Creepers
Full Moon Slaughter
Down The Rabbit Hole: Tales of Insanity

Collections
The Cash Compendium Volume 1 [coming soon]
Website:
www.Facebook.com/pinprickbymatthewcash

DEMON THINGY

JONATHAN BUTCHER

Jonathan Butcher is the twisted bugger responsible for stories such as the novella What Good Girls Do published by The Sinister Horror Company, the short comedy-horror film Stuck which screened at the Bristol Horror Convention 2017, and a host of horrid shorter pieces like The Chocolateman and Cthulhu Cummeth. He has a full-length gangland horror novel set to be released in 2018 called The Children at the Bottom of the Gardden, and is working on a novel about political and religious extremism called Beast of the Earth. Jonathan is a full-blown horror fanatic, as well as a lover of fine ales, good company, and surreal conversation. He also has laser eyes and a third leg growing out of his shoulder.

MORE FROM JONATHAN BUTCHER

Upcoming:

The Children at the Bottom of the Gardden – Burdizzo Books

The Hidebehind – Sinister Horror Company, Black Room Manuscripts 3

Available:

What Good Girls Do – Sinister Horror Company

The Chocolateman – Sinister Horror Company

The Last Hangover – Weird Ales 3 – Knightwatch Press

Flash Fear (editor and contributor) – Knightwatch Press

Cthulhu Cummeth – Dunhams Does Lovecraft – Dunhams Manor Press

The Project – Dark Designs – Shadow Works Publishing

Chagrin – Trapped Within – Eyecue Productions

Gift from a Star – 12 Days: STOCKING FILLERS – Burdizzo Books

OTHER TITLES TO LOOK OUT FOR BY JONATHAN BUTCHER AND MATTHEW CASH

WHAT GOOD GIRLS DO

JONATHAN BUTCHER

She has never left her room.
All she has ever known is pain and abuse.
Until now.

Today, she will breathe fresh air for the first time, feel sunshine against her skin and even witness human kindness.

But she has a point to make – a bleak, violent point – and when she meets her neighbour, Serenity, she finds the perfect pupil.

Forced to endure a lesson distilled from a nightmarish existence Serenity must face unflinching evil, witness the unspeakable, and question her most deeply-held views, until at last she has no choice but to fight for her family's survival.

THE CHOCOLATEMAN

JONATHAN BUTCHER

The Chocolateman: a short story by Jonathan Butcher

"There was a rhyme that some of them said the Chocolateman had whispered to them through the pipes: I'm the one who eats your food, after you've digested it ..."

"Please stop."

"My aim is never to be rude – just to eat your rich chocolate ..."

"Please, I don't like it."

"I'm the Chocolateman, you know, I take my time but I'm never slow..."

"That's enough!"

"Kreb's the name, called one, two, three, Take a dump and there I'll be."

The Sinister Horror Company invites you to wade through the filth of this short story as Jonathan Butcher introduces us to the foulest, most perverse horror villain of the modern age.

DEMON THINGY

PINPRICK

MATTHEW CASH

All villages have their secrets Brantham is no different. Twenty years ago after foolish risk taking turned into tragedy Shane left the rural community under a cloud of suspicion and rumour. Events from that night remained unexplained, memories erased, questions unanswered. Now a notorious politician, he returns to his birthplace when the offer from a property developer is too good to decline. With big plans to haul Brantham into the 21st century, the developers have already made a devastating impact on the once quaint village. But then the headaches begin, followed by the nightmarish visions. Soon Shane wishes he had never returned as Brantham reveals its ugly secret.

`DEMON THINGY`

VIRGIN AND THE HUNTER

MATTHEW CASH

Hi I'm God. And I have a confession to make.

I live with my two best friends and the girl of my dreams, Persephone.

When the opportunity knocks we are usually down the pub having a few drinks, or we'll hang out in Christchurch Park until it gets dark then go home to do college stuff. Even though I struggle a bit financially life is good, carefree.

Well they were.

Things have started going downhill recently, from the moment I started killing people.

KRACKERJACK

MATTHEW CASH

Five people wake up in a warehouse, bound to chairs.

Before each of them, tacked to the wall are their witness testimonies.

They each played a part in labelling one of Britain's most loved family entertainers a paedophile and sex offender.

Clearly revenge is the reason they have been brought here, but the man they accused is supposed to be dead.

Opportunity knocks and Diddy Dave Diamond has one last game show to host and it's a knock out.

DEMON THINGY

KRACKERJACK2

MATTHEW CASH

Ever wondered what would happen if a celebrity faked their own death and decided they had changed their minds?

Two years ago publicly shunned comedian Diddy Dave Diamond convinced the nation that he was dead only to return from beyond the grave to seek retribution on those who ruined his career and tainted his legacy.

Innocent or not only one person survived Diddy Dave Diamond's last ever game show, but the forfeit prize was imprisonment for similar alleged crimes.

Prison is not kind to inmates with those type of convictions and as the sole survivor finds out, but there's a sudden glimmer of hope.

Someone has surfaced in the public eye claiming to be the dead comedian

COMING SOON FROM BURDIZZO BOOKS

DEMON THINGY

THE CHILDREN AT THE BOTTOM OF THE GARDDEN

JONATHAN BUTCHER

At the edge of the coastal city of Seadon there stands a dilapidated farmhouse, and at the back of the farmhouse there is a crowd of rotten trees, where something titters and calls.

The Gardden.

Its playful voice promises games, magic, wonders, lies – and roaring torrents of blood.

It speaks not just to its eccentric keeper, Thomas, but also to the outcasts and deviants from Seadon's criminal underworld. At first they are too distracted by their own tangled mistakes and violent lives to notice, but one by one they'll come: a restless Goth, a cheating waster, a sullen concubine, a perverted drug baron, and a murderous sociopath.

Haunted by shadowed things with coal-black eyes, something malicious and ancient will lure them ever closer. And on a summer's day not long from now, they'll gather beneath the leaves in a place where nightmares become flesh, secrets rise up from the dark, and a voice coaxes them to play and stay, yes yes yes, forever.

FUR

MATTHEW CASH

The old aged pensioners of Boxford are very set in their ways, loyal to each other and their daily routines. With families and loved ones either moved on to pastures new or maybe even the next life, these folk can get dependant on one another.

But what happens when the natural ailments of old age begin to take their toll?

What if they were given the opportunity to heal and overcome the things that make every day life less tolerable?

What if they were given this ability without their consent?

When a group of local thugs attack the village's wealthy Victor Krauss they unwittingly create a maelstrom of events that not only could destroy their home, but everyone in and around it.

Are the old folk the cause or the cure of the horrors?